A Flair for Vegas

A Flair for Vegas

A Sadie Kramer Flair Mystery

Deborah Garner

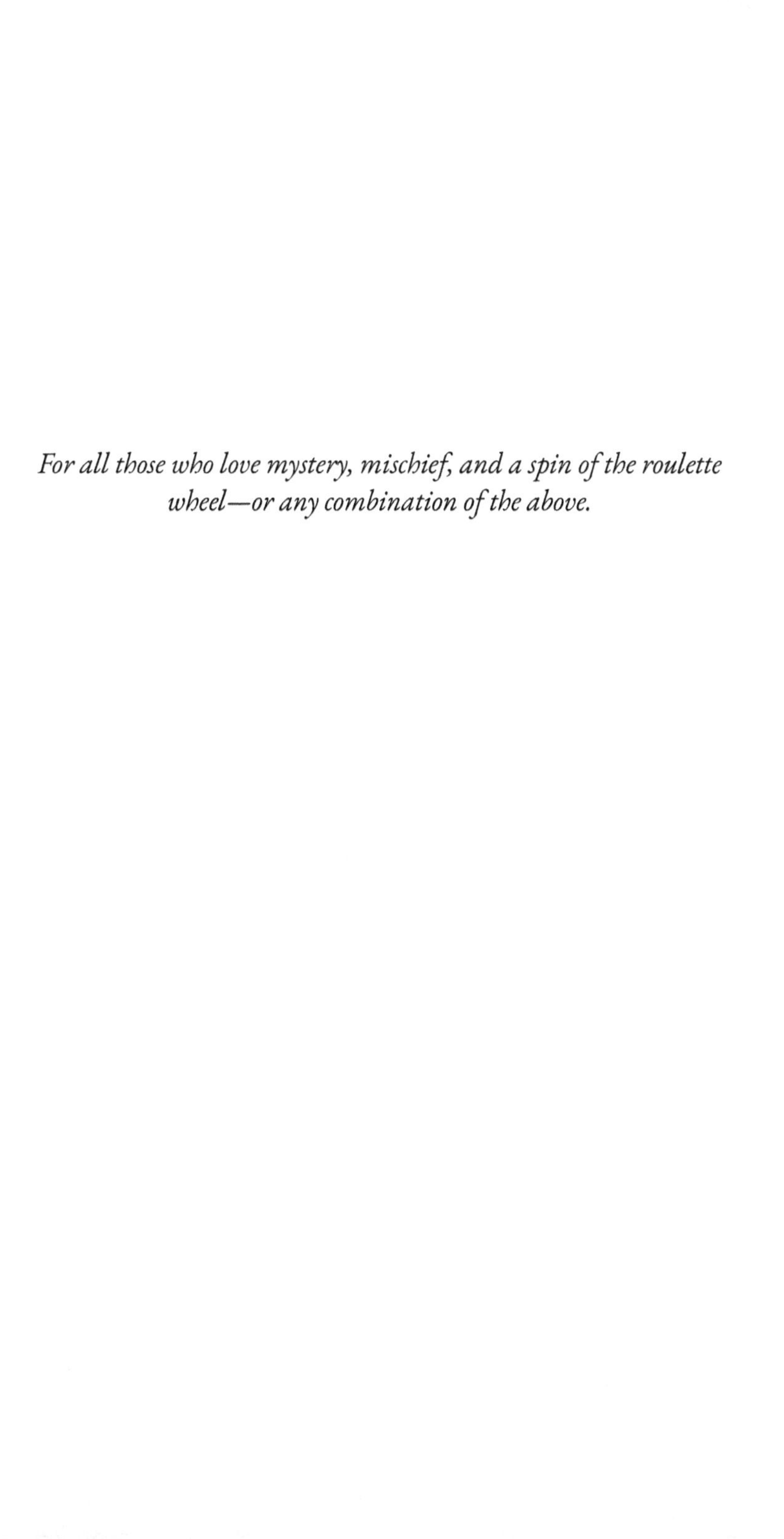

For all those who love mystery, mischief, and a spin of the roulette wheel—or any combination of the above.

The Paige MacKenzie Mystery Series
Above the Bridge
The Moonglow Café
Three Silver Doves
Hutchins Creek Cache
Crazy Fox Ranch
Sweet Sierra Gulch

The Moonglow Christmas Series
Mistletoe at Moonglow
Silver Bells at Moonglow
Gingerbread at Moonglow
Nutcracker Sweets at Moonglow
Snowfall at Moonglow
Yuletide at Moonglow
Starlight at Moonglow
Joy at Moonglow
Evergreen Wishes at Moonglow
Angels at Moonglow
Sleigh Bells at Moonglow

ONE

The lobby of the Speakeasy Hotel and Casino seemed to stretch for miles. From the spot where Sadie stood in line to check in, luggage beside her on a slick tiled floor, it was impossible to see walls in any direction. Only the registration desk itself, set against a geometric backdrop typical of Art Deco style, offered the assurance that she hadn't dropped into some sort of infinite universe. And even that was a good distance away, considering a dozen people waited in line before her.

Sadie looked around, hoping to spot her friend. She'd sent Myrtle a text when she'd landed at the airport, knowing her partner in crime for the Vegas getaway had arrived hours earlier and already checked in. *Partner in crime*, Sadie thought. Perhaps this wasn't the best phrase to use to define their friendship. After all, she'd met Myrtle at a crime scene, a beachside hotel in Southern California. Not that it had been a crime scene when they'd met, and not that they had anything to do with the crime, aside from solving it, that is. The shared happenstance of being in the wrong place at the wrong time was what started their friendship.

The Las Vegas trip had been Myrtle's idea. It wasn't Sadie's first trip to Sin City. The popular vacation spot was an easy hop from San Francisco, where Sadie lived and ran her fashion boutique, Flair. She didn't consider herself a Vegas-type person, not being a gambler, but the city appealed to her in a change-of-pace sort of way. The bright neon lights cast an exciting glow over the city at night, making evening walks invigorating, and the extravagant outdoor landscaping of waterfalls and lush gardens made daytime wandering an adventure as well. And there was no better place for people-watching, one of Sadie's favorite activities.

Myrtle, on the other hand, had never been to Las Vegas. So when the two women had discussed possibilities for a girls' weekend out, it scored high on the list of options. The location itself was a reasonable meeting place with Sadie coming from the west coast and Myrtle from the Midwest. And the city offered plenty to do without even setting foot inside a casino—shows, for example, and shopping. There was always shopping.

A yip from Sadie's tote bag brought her back from these rambling thoughts. She slipped a hand into an outside pocket and pulled a tiny treat out, which she dropped inside. "There you go, Coco," she whispered to the bag's opening. "We'll be in our room soon." Coco, the petite Yorkie inside, was a good travel companion but lacked patience with long lines, even with the cushy pillow inside the tote as a comfortable resting place.

Sadie stepped forward as the line moved closer to the registration desk. With only seven people in front of her and three agents assisting with guest arrivals, she knew she'd be checked in soon. She dropped another treat into her tote and checked her phone, delighted to see a return text from Myrtle.

Glad you're here! I'm in my room, but I'll meet you downstairs.

Sadie looked around and spotted a coffee kiosk. A carpeted area in front of it offered an array of couches, chairs, and tables. A few seats were unoccupied, and the line for counter service was shorter than the one she stood in now.

How about that coffee kiosk in the center of the lobby? Sadie sent the text and moved forward again, pleased to see she was only three people away from the registration desk now.

Perfect, Myrtle replied. *See you there.*

Sadie stepped forward as the person in front of her moved up. Almost immediately she stepped forward again when a second desk clerk called her over with a carefully delivered, "May I help the next guest in line?"

"Yes!" Sadie exclaimed as she rolled her luggage over to the counter and handed a pleasant-looking woman in her thirties a sheet of paper with her hotel reservation on it. She'd found while traveling over the years that it often saved time to have the printed confirmation ready to present.

"Welcome to the Speakeasy Hotel and Casino, Ms. Kramer," the woman said. A name tag with the hotel logo on it identified her as Cassie.

Sadie waited while the desk clerk looked up the reservation on a computer screen and then pulled a check-in packet from a file bucket holding many of the same. The woman presented the packet to her, pointing out coupons for discounts at shops and restaurants located inside the hotel. A map of the hotel's interior was neatly tucked inside the packet, along with two precoded keys.

"This will be your room," Cassie said, pointing to the room number without saying it out loud. This was a gesture that Sadie appreciated. There was no need to announce her room location to others. Her first impression of the hotel, already high, went up another notch at this professional nod to guest safety. "And here is the Wi-Fi code and also your password to get into the bar, the Blind Pig. If there's anything we can do to help make your stay more enjoyable, please let us know."

"Thank you, I will," Sadie said. She took the packet of keys and information and stepped away from the desk to allow the next person in line to approach. Pulling her luggage with one hand while clutching her hotel packet and tote bag in her other hand, she made her way through the crowded lobby to the coffee kiosk, where she found Myrtle waiting in the sitting area.

"Sadie! There you are!" Myrtle jumped up from a plush chair, one of two that matched each other. The second chair held a sweater and several magazines. Sadie guessed correctly that it was her friend's way of saving a place for her. After exchanging greetings and hugs, Myrtle whisked the items out of the chair and both women sat down.

"You look fabulous, Myrtle!" Sadie rarely met anyone with the same carefree, fun sense of style that she had herself, but Myrtle was a fashion diva after her own heart. The emerald-green dress with a martini-glass print was frivolous and classy at the same time. Chunky black bangles and a black-and-silver twenties-style knotted bead necklace added just the right touch. The combination of clothing and accessories was perfect with Myrtle's silver hair, which sported a bow-shaped hair clip with Swarovski crystals.

"So do you!" Myrtle exclaimed as her eyes surveyed Sadie's blue-and-white-striped tunic, white slacks, and chunky blue tagua nut necklace. "I can't believe we're both here. This was such a great idea!"

"The greatest! And I love this place with its roaring twenties atmosphere!"

"I know!" Myrtle said. "Even a password to get into the bar. Very authentic. I hope we don't forget it." She lowered her voice and whispered, "How could we forget something as silly as 'giggle water' anyway?"

Sadie laughed. "I doubt it's actually needed, but it adds to the ambiance." She stood back up. "I'm getting us both coffees. What can I order for you? I'm going for some kind of iced something or other with whipped cream and whatever else they can put on it."

"Make that two of the same. That sounds delicious," Myrtle said. She reached for her purse, but Sadie brushed the offer of payment away.

"My treat," Sadie insisted. "Just save our seats. We'll lose them if we both get up." She glanced around the lobby, her suspicions confirmed. The hotel was getting busier, and several customers stood near the coffee kiosk, scanning the area for places to sit.

Clutching her tote bag securely, Sadie walked to the counter, pleased to find herself next in line after two college-aged girls. Flirtatious banter flew back and forth between the girls and a barista of similar age behind the counter, who to his credit filled their orders promptly.

"You see, Coco?" Sadie said as she waited for her turn. The Yorkie, hearing her name, stuck her head out of the tote and yipped. "We're on another adventure, this time with Myrtle. And it's Vegas, baby! And you know what they say: What happens in Vegas stays in Vegas!"

A voice interrupted Sadie's animated conversation with Coco as the young man who'd been the object of the girls' attention asked Sadie for her order.

"Two blended iced whatevers with everything on top."

"Frappuccinos?" The young man glanced at Coco, whose head still lingered above the edge of the tote, her eyes admiring a glass canister of almond biscotti.

"Sure," Sadie said. "Whatever you've got. With whipped cream and... what other options do we have?"

"Crushed cookies? Caramel drizzle? Chocolate sprinkles?"

"Yes," Sadie said.

"Yes, which?"

"All of them," Sadie said. "And two biscotti." Coco turned her head, and Sadie could swear the petite canine gave her the evil eye. If it was possible for a Yorkie to frown, Coco tossed that in for good measure. "Better make that three."

Sadie paid for the drinks and biscotti and, juggling all the treats, returned to Myrtle. Myrtle again removed the place-savers from the chair, and Sadie sat down. Distributing the goods— including a tiny piece of biscotti to Coco—she relaxed back against the plush chair and realized it was the first time she'd settled down since departing the plane. She took a sip of the sweet drink, wiped a bit of whipped cream off her nose with a napkin, and addressed Myrtle.

"Gosh, where do we even start? There's so much to do here."

She took another sip and again tidied up a lingering spot of whipped cream. Myrtle did the same, and they both laughed.

"I booked a spa treatment as soon as I arrived," Myrtle said. "There was just one massage opening, and I wanted to make sure it didn't get booked. And I was able to snag tickets to the show tonight, the one right here at the hotel."

"Really? *Bugsy's Juice Joint*?" Sadie said. "How did you manage that? I thought that show has been sold out for months." She'd read about it in a travel magazine on the flight. The gentleman in the seat next to her had said he'd tried to get tickets but to no avail.

Myrtle looked around and lowered her voice. "They were given to me by a couple in the elevator. Well, by the man, actually. He said their plans for the evening had changed and they didn't want to waste the tickets."

Sadie quirked an eyebrow. "Wow. That was a lucky break. This is supposed to be a great production—showgirls, dancers, live music, award-winning set—the whole works."

"You're up for it then?"

"Absolutely!" Sadie exclaimed. "We're on vacation. Let's live it up!"

The drinks finished, Sadie picked up her hotel packet and looked inside. "I'd better get to the room and settle in. At least get rid of this luggage."

"What floor are you on?" Myrtle asked.

"Fourth floor." Sadie turned the packet so Myrtle could read the room assignment.

"Great!" Myrtle exclaimed. "Same here. I think our rooms are next to each other! The numbers are only two digits apart. That means the same side of the hallway, facing inside. Nice view of the atrium."

Sadie stood, disposed of her empty cup as well as Myrtle's, and grabbed the handle of her luggage. "In that case, lead the way!"

Two

Sadie set her suitcase down by the closet, placed her tote bag on a stylish chair in the corner of the hotel room, and lifted Coco out, snuggling her against her chest while she looked around. The spacious spread offered a king-sized bed, an expanded dresser that housed a compact refrigerator, a table that could also function as a desk, and two wing-backed chairs situated near a large window. The decor was elegant but not ostentatious, mostly rich gold and brown tones accented with touches of red—a pillow here, a vase there. Framed posters of films from the 1920s and 1930s graced the walls: Buster Keaton in *Go West,* Greta Garbo in *Mata Hari,* and Jackie Cooper in *The Champ.*

"Maybe we should just move in, Coco. What do you think?" She tipped the pup's head up to ask the question, and Coco yipped her usual indecipherable answer. *If only I spoke Yorkie,* Sadie thought as she lowered Coco to the floor and reached for the folding travel "palace" that always accompanied them on trips.

Sadie watched attentively as Coco made the rounds of the room, an inspection filled with both sniffing and pondering. Coco was superbly obedient when it came to canine training and manners, but Sadie always kept an eye on her in unfamiliar settings to make sure there were no slips from respecting interior spaces.

Seemingly satisfied with the newfound digs, Coco retreated to the open door of her travel palace, stepped inside, and curled up on the velvet pillow. She'd always been fond of the glorified kennel, but then again, why wouldn't she be? It was hardly the everyday, ordinary crate. The decked-out canine accommodation featured a plush velvet-pillowed floor and additional accessories, which Sadie now pulled from her suitcase—china food and water bowls, an extra velvet pillow, and a few high-quality toys, including Coco's favorite red lobster.

A knock on what sounded like the room's wall drew Sadie's attention. She turned toward the tapping, realized it was from a door to the next room, and hurried over to open it. *Myrtle's room!* She twisted the dead bolt and opened the door. Myrtle, having done the same, stood there, beaming.

"Connecting doors!" Sadie exclaimed. "How convenient!"

"Just like a suite. Come see my room." Myrtle stepped back, and Sadie entered, finding a room just like hers, a mirror image of sorts. The decor, right down to the bedding and art on the walls, was identical, with the exception of different titles for the posters: Clara Bow in *Wings* and Mary Pickford in *Coquette*. Only the direction of the furnishings was reversed.

"You have movie posters too," Sadie noted, finding it fascinating to see more movie history portrayed.

"Yes!" Myrtle exclaimed. "I especially love the one with Douglas Fairbanks in *The Thief of Baghdad*."

"And we both have a fabulous view, don't you think?" Sadie said, moving over to the window. "I'm so glad we got rooms that face in. The street side would be noisy, and we wouldn't have this gorgeous view to enjoy."

Myrtle followed, and both women looked down at the lush landscaping in the atrium below. The garden setting featured palm trees, flowering bushes, and terra-cotta benches. Meandering walkways allowed guests to stroll through the enchanting area.

"There's a light show down there at night—one at six and one at eight," Myrtle said. "It lasts about ten minutes. We should be able to see at least one while we're here." She turned to Sadie. "You do want to see *Bugsy's Juice Joint* tonight, right?"

Sadie nodded enthusiastically. "Of course! It would be silly to waste the show tickets. And it's a great excuse to dress up!"

"My thinking exactly," Myrtle said. "I brought the perfect outfit just in case something special came up." She hustled to the room's closet and pulled out a flashy yellow dress with three-quarter sleeves. A fuchsia sash hung casually from side loops at the waist. To top it off, Myrtle held up a jacket with a scalloped hemline that matched the sash.

"Exquisite," Sadie gushed as she reached out to feel the soft fabric of the sash. "I love that color combination. It's very festive. I brought something dressy as well. We'll be the best-dressed guests at the show, I'm sure."

A double yip drew their attention to the doorway between the rooms, where Coco now stood, a questioning expression on her petite face. Sadie rushed over and scooped her up, apologizing for leaving her out of the conversation. However, in Sadie's defense, Coco had been contentedly curled up on the velvet pillow in the travel palace.

"What time does the show start?" Sadie set Coco down, cautioning her to be good. The pup proceeded to cruise around, inspecting, sniffing, and apparently approving of Myrtle's room.

"I think eight, but let's make sure." Myrtle picked up an envelope from the top of the dresser and opened it. As she pulled out two tickets, one fell to the floor.

"Wow!" Sadie exclaimed as she reached down and picked the ticket up.

"What is it?" Myrtle asked absentmindedly as she checked for the show's starting time.

Sadie moved closer to the window, where the light was better. She lifted the ticket up, inspecting it. "These were expensive! I can't believe they just gave them away!"

"You're right," Myrtle said, eyes widening as she saw the price. She handed Sadie the other ticket and envelope. "You hang on to them."

"These are VIP seats, Myrtle," Sadie pointed out. "That's why they were so expensive." She held the tickets up in the air and pointed to the VIP designation.

"Interesting," Myrtle said, sinking into one of the room's plush chairs. "The man didn't seem concerned at all about giving them away. In fact, he seemed relieved to get rid of them."

Sadie took a seat in the chair opposite Myrtle, and Coco jumped up in her lap. "Well, that's strange. Maybe he was just grateful the tickets wouldn't go to waste."

"Maybe." Myrtle leaned back, seemingly unconvinced. "I really didn't think anything of it at the time. I just thought they were being nice, and I happened to be lucky enough to be in the elevator. But now... no, I'm just imagining things." She shook her head as if trying to toss her thoughts away.

"Like what?" Sadie said. "Imagining what?"

Myrtle leaned forward and lowered her voice. Sadie thought it an overly dramatic stance, considering no one else was in the room, but she chose to overlook it. After all, she had plenty of quirks herself.

"Now that I think about it, the woman was really miffed with her husband—or whoever the man was—for giving the tickets away."

"Why do you say that?"

"Because she kind of shushed him when he offered them to me." Myrtle tapped a manicured index finger against her forehead as if trying to remember the exchange more clearly. "And her eyes bugged out. You know, the way they do when people are shocked about something."

"Maybe she really wanted to go to the show," Sadie suggested. "Or maybe she thought he should sell them instead of giving them away, since they were pricey. You know how sometimes you can buy tickets outside a venue from people? Or she was upset with him for not discussing it with her before giving them away. Who knows?"

Myrtle shrugged. "You're probably right. It's easy to imagine things in retrospect."

Or to remember them more accurately, like suspicious behavior, Sadie thought.

"I should take this little ragamuffin out for a stroll," Sadie said. She patted Coco on the head, then stood up. Coco yipped in agreement, having heard the word "out." It ranked right up there with "walk" and "go" on the pup's list of favorite words. Along with "treat" and "dinner," of course.

Sadie headed for the open doors between the two rooms. "You're welcome to join us."

Myrtle shook her head. "Thanks, I'd love to, but I have that spa appointment in less than an hour. I don't want to be late. In fact, I think I'll head there now and spend a few minutes in the sauna. Should I see if they have another opening? I could text you if they do."

"No, thanks," Sadie said. "Maybe I'll check into it tomorrow. Right now I think Coco and I have some window shopping to do. Or *more* than just window shopping. I see the possibility of some purchasing too."

"Smart," Myrtle said. "You never know when a must-have item will catch your eye. Let me know if you find a great shop. I plan to do some retail damage myself while here."

Sadie laughed. "Catch up with you later? Dinner before the show?" Getting a nod of approval from Myrtle, Sadie stepped back into her room and closed the door. She clipped Coco's leash to her collar, placed her in the tote bag, and headed out to explore.

THREE

The Las Vegas scene was just as energetic as Sadie remembered. Tourists ambled along the sidewalks, some carrying bags bearing newly purchased items, others chatting on cell phones, still others craning their necks to look up at extravagant buildings that looked as if they'd been dropped in from other countries or even distant planets.

"There's no place quite like Vegas," Sadie said out loud. She intended her comment for Coco, but it drew an unexpected response from nearby.

"You can say that again, sweetie."

Sadie turned toward the voice, finding a tall, slender woman in jeans and a faded black T-shirt with a rhinestone kitten on the front. Waves of light brown hair flowed down from below a white bandanna that wrapped tightly across the woman's forehead and tied at the nape of her neck. She wore no makeup that Sadie could tell, and no jewelry other than two fairly nondescript earrings.

"There's no place quite like Vegas," Sadie repeated, feeling quite clever. After all, the woman *had* said she could say it again.

"I suppose I deserved that." The woman laughed.

Coco, not to be left out of the encounter, stuck her head out of Sadie's tote bag, eyed the woman curiously, and then ventured a yipped hello. The greeting elicited several cooing remarks. "What a darling… just adorable… love that cute face!"

"This is Coco," Sadie said, introducing the petite canine properly. "And I'm Sadie, smart-aleck tourist."

"Pleased to meet you both. I'm Josie, smart-aleck local." She reached out to pat Coco on the head. "Coco reminds me of a dog I had as a child, a little terrier named Rusty."

"That's a great name," Sadie said.

"Thanks. I usually just called him Rascal though. He was full of mischief."

Sadie laughed. "That certainly applies to this one." She looked down at Coco and could almost swear the pup beamed with pride.

"I thought I'd check out some boutiques," Sadie said, then wondered why she'd even made that comment other than the fact it was something to say. Any day in Vegas was a good day for shopping. She could have stuck with a cliché weather tidbit. In addition, Josie not only didn't have any shopping bags but didn't even have a purse. She obviously wasn't on her way to boutiques.

Josie nodded politely. "There are some great shops around. I'm just on a work break." She sighed and stretched her neck from side to side. Sadie noted that her neck was long, as were her legs.

"Oh, what an exciting place to work, here along the Strip," Sadie exclaimed. "I love the buzz of activity. I'm staying at the Speakeasy Hotel and Casino. It has such a fun roaring twenties vibe. Plenty of energy."

Josie smiled in that way people smile to be polite in the face of mundane chatter. "Yes. I would say, 'you could say that again,' but then…"

Sadie raised one hand and made a zipping motion across her lips, then reversed it to unzip them before speaking. "I like the energy there. It's a perfect place for a 'girls' weekend out' as my friend and I are calling it. We even have tickets to the show there tonight."

"Really? Well, then you'll probably spot me in the chorus line."

Suddenly Josie's long legs and long neck took on a new perspective. A showgirl, of course! "Oh, you're in the show! How exciting!" Sadie said. "I've always thought it would be thrilling to be in a show like that."

"At times it is," Josie said. "Other times it's just a job. You know, something to pay the bills. Sometimes emotions run high, and lately... well, there's no point in going there. Speaking of the job, I'd better get back. Seth, our director, said to take ten and I've taken nine and a half. He's sure to throw one of his tantrums. Showbiz temperament."

Sadie picked up on a contradiction in Josie's words, one that balanced criticism with a bit of admiration. "Sounds like he's not exactly fun to work for."

"You can say... no, I'd better not say that!" Josie laughed but then turned serious. "I just do my best and keep my distance. Otherwise, we just end up arguing about the damage he's doing to my career."

"Really?" Sadie couldn't help but be curious. "In what way?"

Josie huffed. "He's constantly turning me down for all the better roles, the solo parts, that kind of thing. I'm sick of arguing with him about it."

"That would be frustrating," Sadie agreed.

"And now I'm officially late." Josie patted Coco on the head, waved to Sadie, and rushed off toward the hotel.

"Wasn't that fun, Coco?" Sadie said, the thrill of meeting the dancer mixing with an odd feeling of discomfort. Perhaps hearing the inside details from Josie put a slight damper on the event. But it made sense that what the audience sees and what goes on behind the curtain could be two very different scenarios.

Sadie checked the Yorkie's leash, confirmed it was securely attached to her collar, and then continued walking, the petite pup trotting along beside her. "We met a real Las Vegas showgirl. I probably should have asked for her autograph. Maybe we can get one tonight." This was a plan not entirely out of the realm of possibility, seeing as their VIP tickets included backstage passes and a meet and greet with the cast. Yes, that is what she'd do. She'd have Josie sign the program for the show. "Remind me to take a pen, Coco."

This last thought caused Sadie to pause. The hotel was pet-friendly, but that didn't mean the theater was. Why hadn't she thought about this earlier? Although she was allowed to leave Coco in the room for short periods of time if crated—a rule surely designed to encourage gambling since pets other than service dogs were not allowed in the casino—the show would likely last a couple of hours. Maybe she'd ask the front desk if they knew someone who could pet-sit. The other option was to sneak Coco into the theater in her tote bag. This was something she'd certainly done in the past, and Coco was extremely well-behaved at such times. There was always the chance of a random yip, but that was probably her best option.

Knowing Myrtle would be tied up at the spa for a while, Sadie wandered on until one shop window caught her attention. A mannequin decked out in a coral outfit seemed to shout Sadie's name. Not one to turn down a shopping suggestion, even from an inanimate plastic form, she noted the LAS VEGAS LILY's sign above the door, settled Coco back in her tote, and stepped inside.

Sadie had been to many shops while traveling, feeling purchases while on trips constituted practical souvenirs of a sort. At least that was one excuse. This particular shop reminded her of many she'd encountered over the years but with a Vegas flair. Racks of T-shirts featured glittered lettering with LAS VEGAS in bold fonts. Others boasted the well-known slogan, WHAT HAPPENS IN VEGAS STAYS IN VEGAS and variations of the same: VEGAS? I'LL NEVER TELL plus others like MARRIED BY ELVIS, and ONE CASINO, TWO CASINO, THREE CASINO, POOR.

The shop was crowded with tourists but not so crowded that the dressing rooms were all occupied. Sadie pulled two blouses from a rack displaying the style in the window, one in her usual size and another one size larger just in case any recent chocolate infusions had added a few pounds. She grabbed a pair of silky black slacks off another rack—after all, she only had three similar pairs at home—and entered an unoccupied dressing room. Rooms to either side of hers showed legs below the partition walls. Comments flowed between the two, leaving Sadie sandwiched between two sides of a conversation, chatter flowing over her head.

"Too tight," one voice said.

"Try a four."

An exasperated sigh followed from the first who'd issued the initial comment. "I'm always a two! These must run small!"

Sadie looked at the tags on her items, debating whether to try on the size twelve first or the fourteen. She opted for the larger one, thinking it would feel better to move down a size than up if it didn't fit. As she slipped the coral blouse on, the conversation between the two dressing rooms continued.

"Could you believe that argument last night?"

"Truly ridiculous. People should know better than to fight in the buffet area even if they are tucked away in a booth."

"I don't know why she even hangs out with him anymore. They broke up ages ago."

"Money, honey." The sound of a zipper followed.

"I doubt it. Show directors don't exactly make bank."

A woman's laugh. "Unless he gets lucky at that blackjack table."

"He's an idiot. He shouldn't gamble where he works. There are plenty of other places he could go. This is Las Vegas after all."

Hangers clattered together. "Not where he has an in with a dealer like Stacey."

"The floozie with the blue streak in her platinum hair?"

"That's the one."

"You believe those rumors?"

"Josie does. I'm sure that's what they were arguing about."

Sadie's ears perked up. *Josie?* Were these girls also in the show? She listened to see if anything more specific followed, but the girls gathered their clothing choices—leaving a mess behind, Sadie was quite certain—and left the dressing room area, chattering on their way out but without further mention of names.

"Well, *that* was interesting!" she whispered to Coco. Gathering her selections—the size twelve had been just fine as well as a long-sleeved T-shirt with multicolored sequins spelling out LAS VEGAS along one sleeve—she quickly paid for her purchases and hustled back to the hotel, eager to discuss the events with Myrtle.

FOUR

After tapping for permission and receiving a welcoming reply, Sadie opened the adjoining doors and stuck her head inside Myrtle's room. "I'm back from shopping, and I have tales to tell!" Sadie stepped back into her own room, set her tote bag down on one of the plush chairs by the window, and let Coco roam free.

"That spa here is simply divine!" Myrtle called out.

"Can't wait to hear about it," Sadie called back and then chuckled. *Just like kids yelling from one room to the next.* She filled Coco's water bowl and set it inside the pup's travel palace, leaving the kennel's door open.

"You must book some treatments while we're here," Myrtle said when Sadie finally joined her. "This spa is fabulous. Go for the hot stone massage and a raspberry sugar scrub." Her bathrobe-clad figure lay sprawled across the bed in her room. Propped up on her elbows, she flipped the page of a magazine and looked up.

Sadie chortled. "I prefer my sugar intake to be in the form of chocolate. Couldn't I just pop a few raspberry truffles instead?"

"You don't know what you're missing." Myrtle smiled as she looked back down and flipped another page. "Besides, there are no calories in the sugar scrub. At least I don't think so... unless the skin absorbs..."

"Don't," Sadie said, stopping her friend before the sentence could continue. "That's the type of question that keeps me up at night."

Myrtle responded with a sympathetic hum. "I understand. I still ponder the chicken and the egg question."

"That appointment was entertaining too," Myrtle said. "The therapist—her name is Tawny—is quite the chatterbox. I heard all sorts of inside tidbits ranging from clandestine relationships to who just had cosmetic surgery. We're vacationing in the middle of a real-life soap opera." She sat up and set the magazine aside. "Any dinner ideas?"

Sadie settled into a chair and patted her lap. Coco jumped up, curled into a fuzzy ball of fur, and made a contented cooing sound. "Something simple tonight," she suggested. "Before we go to the show."

"I was thinking the buffet here would be convenient," Myrtle said. "Gatsby's Grill."

"Oh yes! The buffet!"

Myrtle eyed her curiously. "I meant easy rather than earth-shatteringly exciting."

Sadie shifted in her chair, and Coco repositioned herself accordingly. "Of course. It just reminded me to tell you about a conversation I overheard in a dressing room today."

"About the buffet? Is it recommended?"

"No idea," Sadie said. "But a buffet's a buffet. I like them. You can choose whatever you want and leave whatever you don't want."

"Good point," Myrtle said. "So what did you hear in the dressing room?"

"Two girls were discussing an argument they heard between the show's director and someone else. It sounds like it was heated, at least enough so that they shouldn't have the argument in the buffet area."

"Who was the other person he was arguing with?"

"Sounded like a blackjack dealer that he has some kind of in with. They said Josie—that's a showgirl I met outside—believes some sort of rumors."

"You met a showgirl? How fun."

"Yes, she seemed nice. Legs that went on for days! Coco reminded her of a dog she had as a child."

"So what kind of rumors were they talking about?"

Sadie shrugged. "I don't know any specifics."

Myrtle perked up. "Ooh, it's starting to sound juicy. Director, blackjack dealer, showgirl, rumors, arguments. Maybe we'll have even more entertainment on this getaway than we expected."

Coco yipped, as if excited by the possibility.

"Don't get any ideas, Coco," Sadie said, giving the Yorkie's head an affectionate tousle. "The last time you got intrigued by a theatre performance, you ended up in the show."

Myrtle smirked. "My kind of dog."

"Anyway," Sadie continued, "I get the impression the director isn't too popular. The dressing room girls didn't sound like fans, and Josie said he has a showbiz temperament."

"Maybe Josie's the one he was arguing with," Myrtle suggested.

Sadie thought back to the conversation. "Could be. She sounded very frustrated that he wasn't giving her solo parts. Or he was arguing with the blackjack dealer they mentioned."

"Or someone else in the cast or a girlfriend, a wife, a sister, or maybe we should just go have dinner." Myrtle walked to the closet and pulled out black pants and a silver tunic with ruffled bell sleeves and rhinestones around the neckline. She held the combo up in front of her. "What do you think? I have metallic silver flats and a black pearl necklace to go with it."

"Spiffy! I'll get changed and meet you in the hallway in twenty."

"Perfect," Myrtle said.

Sadie, impressed with Myrtle's outfit but not to be outdone, retreated to her room with Coco, took a quick shower, applied a smattering of makeup, and donned a leopard-print pantsuit with gold buttons shaped like elephants along the front of the jacket. She changed Coco's collar to match and clipped a barrette atop the petite canine's head that she'd made with the extra button that came inside the jacket. Sliding treats into the side pocket of her tote bag, she placed Coco inside and met up with Myrtle in the hallway.

"You have the tickets?" Sadie asked as they started walking toward the elevators.

Myrtle patted the silver evening bag that hung from her shoulder. Sadie noticed her friend had added a fluffy sequined black bow to her outfit, pulling her silver hair back dramatically above one ear. A pair of dice earrings with black crystal dots dangled from her earlobes. Rarely had Sadie been so impressed with someone's fashion sense.

The lobby was buzzing with energy when they arrived downstairs, and the buffet was crowded. Many, it appeared from the upscale dress throughout, seemed to have had the same idea they had: an easy preshow meal. Sadie and Myrtle looked around while waiting in line, wondering if they'd even find a place to sit.

"Look at the list of events," Myrtle said, indicating a standing hotel poster. "An Art Deco exhibition in one of the conference halls, the salute to the roaring twenties atrium light show, a Charleston dance lesson, and a ragtime to jazz live music presentation nightly in the lobby."

"So many choices." Sadie sighed. "I do love the music from that period. We should check that out." She tapped her foot and hummed a few bars of "Ain't Misbehavin'."

Myrtle laughed. "I don't know about you. I plan to misbehave all I want on this trip. But I agree we'll have to catch the lobby music at least once. And a Charleston lesson would be a blast. That's always looked like fun. All that energy!"

Sadie laughed. "Speak for yourself! My knees hurt just thinking about it!"

"Come on," Myrtle chided. "Where's your sense of adventure? Vacations are all about trying new things."

Finally they spotted customers leaving in the middle of the room. They made a beeline to the table and hovered over it as an employee cleaned it off, set wrapped utensils down, and dropped a ticket on the table to show it was occupied.

"I was hoping to see the couple who gave me the tickets," Myrtle said, looking around. "I wanted to thank them, but they don't appear to be here."

"They must have made other plans when they decided not to go to the show. Since we ended up with the tickets, I mean."

"When *he* decided not to go to the show," Myrtle pointed out. "The woman didn't seem to have any say in the matter."

Sadie nodded as she hung her jacket on the back of her chair and eyed the expansive buffet, debating a plan of attack. Slinging her tote bag over her shoulder, she nodded toward a section with a shorter line than others and headed across the room, Myrtle just behind.

"Pasta!" Sadie said to Myrtle once they were close enough to see. She waited for the person in front of her to take a plate, then picked up two and handed one to Myrtle. "A perfect place to start! Look at these trays: lasagna, manicotti, spaghetti and meatballs, garlic cheese bread, and three kinds of pizza."

"I'm limiting myself to one item here," Myrtle said, looking down the row of food sections. "There are too many other choices. I'd rather make a sampler plate and try different things. Plus you know there'll be a dessert bar."

"Excellent point," Sadie said as she limited herself to a modest serving of lasagna and one slice of pizza. She moved along the buffet stations, adding selections at the salad bar, the Asian food offerings, and a tempting spread of barbecued and fried foods, where she limited herself to a handful of popcorn chicken and a few fries. Myrtle made similar choices, and both women returned to their table.

Sadie placed her tote bag in her lap and casually dropped a

piece of popcorn chicken inside. A tiny yip of thanks followed. "Must share the wealth," she explained to Myrtle, who laughed.

Thirty minutes, one tiramisu, and one apple crisp later, Sadie and Myrtle dabbed their mouths with napkins, placed them on the table, and announced surrender. Leaving a tip for the server who had refilled their water glasses and removed empty plates, they gathered their jackets and purses and headed out.

FIVE

The Speakeasy Theater boasted luxurious seating under an expansive ceiling that Sadie estimated to be at least sixty feet high, possibly more considering a balcony section. Not having considered what VIP seating might be, it came as a surprise when a smartly dressed usher escorted them to a section of roped-off rows up front. They were even more surprised when they took their places in the first row, finding swag bags on each seat.

"Ooh!" Myrtle took a seat and rummaged through her bag of treats. "Look at these goodies: imported Swiss chocolate, a coupon for a complimentary spa treatment, a backstage pass, and more." She held up a crystal shot glass and watched the auditorium lights reflect off the production name etched on its surface. "No wonder that woman seemed upset when the man handed me the tickets. I would have been too."

"For losing the chocolate alone," Sadie noted. She peeked into her own swag bag to make sure that it also held her favorite addiction. "Don't you find it odd that she didn't know he was going to give them away?"

"I'm not sure he even knew he was going to. It seemed impulsive, almost as if he held something that had suddenly started to burn his hands. He looked flustered, like he just wanted to get rid of them and get out of there."

"Interesting." Sadie glanced around and noted others arriving, though not many settled in the same front section where they'd been seated. Turning back to face the stage, she opened a show program they'd picked up on the way into the theater and flipped through the pages. "Look," she said, pointing to a small photo in the middle of others. "That's Josie, the girl I met today."

Myrtle leaned over to check out the photo. "The one whose name was mentioned in the dressing room?"

"Yes," Sadie said. "Maybe we'll get a chance to see her after the show. That backstage pass might do it. I could introduce you." She checked her swag again, pleased but not surprised to see she also had a backstage pass. Their VIP gifts were identical.

"Ooh, that would be great!" Myrtle exclaimed, rubbing her hands together. "I bet she knows some juicy behind-the-scenes gossip."

Sadie laughed. "I'm sure she does. She definitely gave me the impression that tempers fly at rehearsals. I imagine there's always some inside drama with productions like this." A tiny yip followed, and Sadie nodded toward her tote bag. "Speaking from experience, or maybe that should be 'barking from experience.'" Her voice trailed off as a man with a headset stepped out on the stage.

"Oh good! Maybe the show's about to start," Myrtle said. She tucked her VIP bag next to one hip and sat up straighter.

"I'm not so sure about that." Sadie frowned as she watched the man walk to the center of the stage, his demeanor professional but shaky. "The lights should be dimming, and they aren't. He looks distraught, don't you think?"

"A little," Myrtle agreed. "Certainly nervous. I wonder what's up?"

"I don't know," Sadie said. "But I have a feeling we're about to find out."

The man, a lanky figure Sadie estimated to be in his midthirties, turned to face the audience. It struck her that he looked somehow diminished against the red curtain backdrop. His black jeans and black shirt made him look even more so. Complete with the black headset, Sadie had the bizarre thought that he looked like an ant.

"Ladies and gentlemen," he began before stopping abruptly. He cleared his throat and continued. "I regret to inform you that we will not be able to proceed with our show tonight. We've had..." Again he stopped, as if struggling for words. "We've had to postpone the opening of our show. I apologize. That's all I can say at this time. Please contact your ticket providers regarding refunds. We thank you for your understanding." Whispers circled the theater as the audience took in the news.

"Well," Myrtle said. "So much for the old adage, 'The show must go on.' I wonder what happened."

"It must be something serious." Sadie watched the man retreat across the stage, touching his headset with one hand as he disappeared into the wings. The dull buzz of conversation that his announcement had triggered grew louder as members of the audience began to gather their evening bags and stylish jackets.

Sadie and Myrtle stood and turned to face the back of the theater but remained by their seats to avoid the crowded aisles filled with people exiting. As the theater emptied, the noise from the audience diminished, and they became aware of sounds from the stage area behind them: hushed chatter, stunned voices, and, from somewhere off to the side, a woman sobbing.

Tempted to linger out of curiosity, their hopes were dashed by the approach of an usher, who kindly offered to escort them out. Sadie recognized the gesture as what it was—a request rather than a suggestion—and she and Myrtle proceeded up the aisle and out into the lobby.

"Well," Sadie said, flipping through the pages of the show program, "I suspect someone in here has run into a little trouble."

"Serious trouble is my guess. Look." Myrtle nodded to several police officers approaching the hotel elevators.

"I say we avoid going back to the room for a bit," Sadie suggested. "At least until we find out what's going on. How does a drink in the bar sound?"

"Like a great idea," Myrtle said. "Maybe we can find something out if we eavesdr... er, I mean listen politely to conversations around us."

"My thoughts exactly."

Sadie and Myrtle headed to the Blind Pig, eager to use the password to get in. Playing along with the Prohibition theme was part of the fun.

"What's with the name?" Myrtle asked, looking at the bar's Art Deco-styled sign.

Sadie smiled, feeling rather pleased to know the answer. Speakeasies were a definite part of San Francisco's history. "That dates back to Prohibition when they couldn't advertise that they were selling alcohol. It was illegal to sell it. They had to come up with a ruse, for example, some other kind of attraction that people were coming to see. Like a blind pig or some other curiosity."

"Aha." Myrtle giggled—appropriately, it seemed—as she whispered the "giggle juice" password to the doorman, and she and Sadie stepped inside. They were not surprised to find the bar crowded with show refugees. Bartenders and cocktail servers alike scurried around, attempting to gather and deliver orders. The crowd occupied every table and chair as well as counter seating. Sadie and Myrtle managed to find standing room in one corner of the swanky establishment. They flagged down a harried server, who took a drink order without even stopping completely.

"I wanted to ask her what happened, but it's too busy," Sadie said, looking around. "This place is packed."

"At least we have two apple martinis on the way," Myrtle pointed out. "Maybe we could ask someone else what's going on."

Sadie nodded, surveying the crowd. "We could, but here's the question: Should we ask someone who's talking, someone who's staring at an untouched drink, or someone who's crying? There seem to be a lot of varied reactions floating around."

"We'll probably get different information from each."

Sadie stood up. "Perfect." She handed her tote bag to Myrtle with instructions to not feed Coco too many pretzels. "Let me see what I can find out."

"I'll catch up with you when the drinks arrive."

Sadie took off toward a table exhibiting a mix of reactions. It couldn't hurt to ask a question or two.

"He was a jerk!" A tall brunette tossed her hair over her shoulder for emphasis.

"Don't you know it's in poor taste to speak ill of the dead?" A twenty-something blonde chastised the woman as she wiped a tear away.

Dead? Sadie's ears perked up.

Based on their six-foot height and heavy makeup, Sadie pegged them both as showgirls, which caused her to look around the room for Josie as the two women launched into a heated argument. Perhaps she could get a less biased account than what was likely to come from the table in front of her.

She spotted Josie against a far wall, a few steps away from the door. Her posture resembled that of someone ready to make a hasty exit, someone keeping close to an escape route but not quite ready to bail. She appeared visibly shaken, and Sadie remembered her comments about getting along better with the director recently. Sadie took advantage of the moment to hurry across the room.

"Josie!" Sadie shouted as if meeting a long-lost friend rather than a stranger she'd only met once. Josie regarded her tentatively before recognizing her. To avoid confusion, Sadie introduced herself again, noting their earlier meeting on the sidewalk.

"This is so shocking," Josie said, her voice shaky.

"What happened anyway?" Sadie said, still at a loss as to what the events actually were. "We were in the audience, waiting for the show to start, when that man with a headset announced that the show wouldn't be opening tonight. He didn't say why, but he was obviously upset."

Josie's fought back tears. "That was our stage manager, Evan. He was barely able to walk out to make that announcement. He'd just been told Seth had been found dead in his hotel room."

"How awful!" Sadie exclaimed. "The show director, right? No wonder so many people are upset." *Some more than others*, she added silently as she glanced around. The differing reactions were intriguing.

Josie nodded. "Seth should have been there already since it was opening night, so Evan went to his room to see what was keeping him."

"And found him..." Sadie couldn't bring herself to finish the sentence. She could only imagine.

Myrtle caught up to them, drinks in hand. She handed one to Sadie, who in turn offered it to Josie, who looked at it blankly and then tossed it back in one gulp.

Sadie leaned closer to Myrtle to be heard over the noisy crowd. "This is Josie, the showgirl I told you about. The show director was found dead in his hotel room right before the show was to start."

"How awful!" Myrtle exclaimed. "No wonder everyone here is upset!"

"Yes," Josie said, handing Sadie the empty glass. "We're all in shock. This is horrible."

"I'm so sorry," Myrtle said.

"Thank you." Josie fought back a sob that Sadie wasn't one hundred percent sure was authentic, exaggerated, or downright acting. "I just hope someone can find out what happened."

Myrtle perked up. "Sadie is fabulous at solving mysteries!"

Sadie shot Myrtle a look, eyebrows raised.

Josie's teary eyes widened. "Really? Then you can figure out what happened?"

"Well, I..."

"Thank you!" Josie said before Sadie could answer. She glanced around the room. "And now I need to check on the other cast members if you'll excuse me."

Sadie watched Josie leave and then turned, eyebrows raised, to Myrtle, who shrugged. A small table opened up near them, and they grabbed it. Sadie plopped into a seat, swiped Myrtle's drink, and took a gulp. "Thanks a lot." Sadie sighed.

"You're welcome!" Myrtle beamed, ignoring Sadie's sarcasm. "Did you find anything else out?" Myrtle dropped a pretzel into the tote bag and handed it back to Sadie.

"Only that there are a lot of mixed reactions here." Sadie looked around and then shuddered. "The assistant director found him. Can you imagine?"

Myrtle shook her head. "Did Josie say anything else?"

"Only that everyone is in shock. She was upset, as you saw."

"Understandably," Myrtle said. "Most everyone seems to be, as can be expected."

Sadie glanced around, noting the women at the first table she'd passed were still arguing. She turned back to Myrtle. "I think it's a little deeper with Josie. She mentioned something when we met about wanting the director to give her better parts."

"Intriguing."

"I don't think anyone knows anything else yet," Sadie said. "Not officially. It's too soon. You saw the police just arriving."

"What about unofficially?" Myrtle quirked an eyebrow.

Sadie's eyes brightened. "I like the way you think, Myrtle! I have an idea. Follow me."

Six

A buzz of activity greeted Sadie and Myrtle as they stepped out of the bar and into the hotel lobby. The few people waiting to check in at the front desk formed a much shorter line than earlier in the day, most guests having arrived in the afternoon and early evening. Those in line now seemed oblivious to the situation, as did others milling around the coffee kiosk or preparing to head to their rooms. A middle-aged couple near the elevator conversed with a police officer who directed them to a different elevator than the one they intended to take. A man in casual dress stood nearby, jotting something down in a notepad.

"Now what?" Myrtle asked as Sadie paused to take stock of the general layout.

Sadie nodded toward the theater and headed in that direction, Myrtle following just behind.

The stately theater doors stood firmly shut, as if daring Sadie and Myrtle to attempt entry. A policeman kept guard at one door, stopping any curious passersby from entering.

"*Ixnay* this idea," Sadie said. She stopped far enough away from the door to not draw the officer's attention.

Myrtle followed suit. "We'll need to find another way in. What about a side entrance?"

"Good idea," Sadie said, looking around. "Let's try over there." She nodded toward a nondescript hallway to one side of the theater. Waiting until the police officer was engaged in conversation, she ambled casually in that direction, Myrtle right behind. Reaching the corner of the theater, they slipped unnoticed into the passageway and picked up their pace, soon arriving at a single door.

"This is the cast entrance," Myrtle said, reading an engraved brass plaque on the wall next to the door.

"Well, I'm feeling quite dramatic today," Sadie said. "How about you?"

"Definitely. I'd say there's drama all around us. Maybe we belong here."

"Excellent point!" Sadie reached for the door handle, pleased to find it unlocked. She and Myrtle both glanced over their shoulders. Noting they were still alone in the hallway, they slipped inside.

The dim lights of the backstage area made Sadie pause in order to let her eyes adjust. Myrtle, equally blinded by the sudden change in illumination, plowed into Sadie, almost causing them both to tumble forward onto a set of stairs. Grabbing at nothing in particular, Sadie grasped a handrail by chance, which kept them both from falling. Myrtle, more prone to colorful language than Sadie, muttered a mild expletive as she regained her balance and stepped back.

"Shh!" Sadie whispered, unsure if others might be backstage. Being discovered would blow their chance to overhear any conversations if crew or cast members were still there. It stood to reason that details might be discussed in the more private location. Besides, how would they justify being in the theater? Sadie had done more than her fair share of sneaking around over the years, and it always took some creative thinking to explain.

Holding the handrail, Sadie and Myrtle made their way up a short flight of five stairs, just enough to bring them to the stage level. Their senses now keen, they took in the musty smell of the heavy velour panels that hung from the ceiling, the close quarters, and the strange silence of the empty backstage area.

As their eyes grew accustomed to the low light, they tiptoed between the hanging curtains, stepping over cables taped to the floor, and around a crowded rack of clothing, presumably for costume changes that were too quick to allow time to return to a dressing room.

The dull glow of a light shining down on a bulletin board caught Sadie's attention. She gestured for Myrtle to follow as she tiptoed over to search the board.

"What are you looking for?" Myrtle whispered.

"Anything," Sadie said. "Maybe a personal note from one cast member to another or an announcement of some sort. Maybe something the director posted himself."

"All I see is a schedule of call times," Myrtle said, perusing the board. "And an ad for a shoe sale."

"Oh!" Sadie checked out the ad in question. "I wonder if they have something in purple."

Myrtle placed her hand on Sadie's arm as a door opened and closed and hushed voices entered the backstage area from the other side of the stage.

Seeing an opportunity to learn more about the director's demise, they pulled back into the wings and took cover behind the wardrobe rack. Footsteps approached, growing louder as they came closer. To Sadie and Myrtle's dismay, they stopped, leaving only a rack of clothes between them. Frozen, they held their breath and listened.

"I'm telling you Seth's death wasn't an accident," a male voice said. "It seems suspicious to me since his hotel room was disturbed."

A second voice, clearly female, gasped. "You're suggesting this was murder? Asher said it looked like he just fell and hit his head."

Asher? Sadie filed the name away for future reference.

"Just because he's saying that doesn't make it true."

"And how do you know his room was disturbed?" the female

voice responded. "Asher's the only one who's been in there. He's the one who found him. The police aren't letting anyone else in."

"Mason in the bar told me."

"How did he know?"

"Maria in housekeeping told him."

"How would *she* know?"

"Sylvia in room service told her."

"And how..."

An exasperated huff from the first voice cut off the new question. "Never mind all that. You know Seth always has—make that *had*, I guess—a shrimp cocktail before any show opening. Room service would have delivered it, and Sylvia was on the schedule, so she would have seen the state of the room."

"Such a weird superstition of his," the second voice said. "Having a shrimp cocktail before each show opening. As if having the same food he ate before his first successful performance years ago would make every performance go well."

"There've been stranger showbiz superstitions, I'm sure. And once people start following one, it's not that easy to break."

"True," the female voice said.

"This is going to hit Stacey pretty hard."

"No more than anyone else. She broke up with him a long time ago. I don't think she was ever that into him anyway." This was followed by a feminine chuckle.

"I bet this has something to do with that financial business," the first voice said.

"What financial business? You mean that whole company of corporate hotshots? Like that guy Bennett, who walks around like he owns all of Vegas?"

Another name to remember, Sadie noted.

"That company Bennett is with practically *does* own all of Vegas. But I'm talking about the new funding for the show. Seth was in on some of those meetings, and he was not happy when he came out. Rumor has it there was some nasty fighting over the new budget, that the deal was about to collapse from him pushing too hard."

"Maybe those rumors are true, maybe not. If they are, it was a mistake from the start for Seth to be involved with the meetings. Everyone knew that."

"Not everyone."

Sounds like Seth didn't, Sadie thought.

Myrtle nudged Sadie once the footsteps had retreated. They heard the stage door open and close, followed by silence. "Strange," she whispered.

"Indeed," Sadie whispered back. She agreed with Myrtle. It was a bit bizarre, not only the money conflicts but also the food angle. But she also knew people tended to develop all kinds of odd superstitions as they went through life. Not only in show business. It was likely the casino was filled with people counting on anything from a favorite piece of jewelry to mismatched socks to roll the dice or deal the cards in their favor. Why couldn't a shrimp cocktail be a good luck charm to the director?

Though perhaps, Sadie thought as she and Myrtle found their way back to the hallway, this time it might have been a very bad luck charm indeed.

Seven

Sadie had just leaned back against the bed's plush pillows, a sip of something indulgent from the mini bar to one side, Coco curled up on the other side, and Agatha Christie's *The Body in the Library* propped before her at the perfect distance for her purple rhinestone reading glasses. She never traveled without a good book, and she could always count on Hercule Poirot to provide a mystery if she couldn't stumble into one herself. But her cozy reading time was soon postponed by a knock on her hotel room's front door.

Curious who it could be—Myrtle would certainly have knocked from her adjoining room—Sadie set the book down and went to find out. She kept the safety chain on the door when she opened it.

"Ms. Kramer?" The man was dressed in that borderline manner one can achieve that's halfway between casual and business attire. He wore jeans with a blue button-down shirt and blazer. He was neither short nor tall, neither slim nor pudgy. With mousy brown hair and matching eyes, he was just about as average as a person could be. She ventured a guess at his age, perhaps forty. She recognized him as the man who'd been writing in a notepad downstairs.

"Yes?" She pressed her face closer to the chain if only to be obstinate. Agatha Christie should not be set aside by this person of, she suspected, no consequence. "May I help you?"

The man nodded. "I believe you can, and I recommend that you do."

Well, that's just rude, Sadie thought. *We're not getting off to the best start.* "Perhaps you could start by telling me who you are and why you're at my door interrupting Hercule Poirot. He has a job to do."

This seemed to give the man pause, as he frowned and appeared to run some unknown number of thought processes through his mind before answering. Finally he cleared his throat and offered an explanation. "Well, I'm not Poirot, though my job might be easier if that were the case. I'm Detective Tanner, and I'm here to ask you to kindly leave the detective work to our department. I assume you're here on vacation. That's the reason most people come to Las Vegas. I advise enjoying your vacation and leaving tonight's unfortunate incident to us. It would be best if you didn't interfere."

Unfortunate incident? Rather an understatement!

The detective produced a badge, which Sadie scrutinized carefully before removing the chain from the door and opening it all of an additional three inches. Coco, who had heard the discussion from the bed and hopped down to join in, stuck her head around the open door and let out a yip of strong proportion, at least as strong as possible for a Yorkie. Detective Tanner looked down and raised his eyebrows. Seemingly unsure how to respond to the petite pup, he raised his gaze back to Sadie.

"And just what makes you think I'm interfering?"

"It may have something to do with you sneaking out of the backstage area earlier," the detective said. "I'm simply asking you to enjoy your stay here as you intended when you decided to visit."

Sneaking? Sadie let out a moderate harrumph. "I hardly think we were sneaking."

"Exiting the backstage area then."

"That does sound better," Sadie said. "I suppose what you're really saying is that we should mind our own business."

"In so many words, yes."

"Well, that's just because you're not aware how helpful I can be." Sadie opened the door wider and stood tall, chin raised. With the exit pathway widened, Coco ventured out and circled the detective's feet. She tilted her head, grasped a shoelace between her teeth, and pulled on it, successfully untying his shoe. Satisfied with the results, she circled around to the other shoe and did the same.

"Somehow I doubt that's the case."

"You can even ask my friend in New Orleans," Sadie said. "He'll back me up." Even as she spoke, she knew this was a tactic that would probably backfire. Her New Orleans detective friend turned beau would be the first to tell her to stay out of it.

"And just who might that be?" Detective Tanner pulled a notepad and pen from his jacket pocket and prepared to write down a name.

"Detective Broussard of the New Orleans Police Department," Sadie explained, trying unsuccessfully to keep the following words from tumbling out of her mouth. "I helped solve a crime there."

"You don't say," the detective said while writing the words down.

"I *do* say," Sadie insisted against her better judgment. "And a few other places too. There was the time in Monterey... Oh wait, he doesn't know about that one. And in Napa Valley... Oh no, he doesn't know about that one either. But he knows about San Francisco. And New Orleans, of course."

Detective Tanner tapped his pen against the notepad and then slipped it back in his pocket. "Have you thought about taking up a hobby at home? Scrapbooking is popular. Or maybe diamond painting, whatever that is. My wife loves both of those. And they keep her out of *trouble*."

Sadie decided not to dignify the suggestions with a response. Although she thought hobbies to be a wonderful use of free time —jigsaw puzzles being a personal favorite—his comments had nothing to do with hobbies and everything to do with getting her to stay out of his way. Eager to end the encounter, she crossed her fingers behind her back and agreed to limit her future pursuits to vacation activities. Coco, back at her side, yipped a backup agreement.

After a few final words and yips all around, Detective Tanner thanked Sadie in advance for staying out of his way—pointlessly, in Sadie's opinion, as she had no intention of doing so—and started down the hall toward the elevator. Sadie noted with amusement that he walked with an unusual gait, moving side to side, not unlike a penguin.

Sadie closed the door after calling out one final comment. "I suggest tying your shoes, Detective. Safety first and all that."

Any intention of going back to reading was thwarted by another knock, this time from the adjoining door to Myrtle's room. Her friend stuck her head in as soon as Sadie replied.

"What was all that about?" Myrtle stepped into the room.

Sadie sighed. "Just a detective telling me to mind my own business."

"In other words, the usual," Myrtle said. "Not that you're going to follow his advice."

Sadie laughed. "Of course not. Where's the fun in that? Besides, he's rather amusing. You should see the way he walks, sort of waddling back and forth. All he needs is a hat, cane, and mustache and he could be Charlie Chaplin. He'd fit right in here."

"Except he's not silent," Myrtle pointed out.

"True." Sadie smiled at Myrtle's reference to Chaplin's history of silent films.

"So now what?"

"I need chocolate," Sadie said, feeling a craving for her favorite addiction. The detective had stressed her out, and this seemed the perfect antidote. This thought left her longing for her friend

Matteo's shop in San Francisco. Cioccolato offered the best gourmet chocolate she'd ever had. But when in Rome, or in this case, Vegas...

"I heard there's a great place just down the street," Myrtle said. "Chocolate Sin."

Sadie felt somewhat of an objection to the name, seeing chocolate as more related to heaven than to that other place. But that wasn't going to stop her from trying out the offerings. Besides, what was a little sin now and then anyway? Especially if it came in the form of chocolate.

"Say no more. Lead the way!" Sadie set her book aside, grabbed a sweater, and got Coco situated in her tote bag while Myrtle ducked into her room to retrieve her purse. Lured by the enticing thought of chocolate treats, they headed out.

THE RICH, LUXURIOUS AROMA OF CHOCOLATE WAFTED over Sadie and Myrtle as they stepped into Chocolate Sin. A long line at the counter indicated the popularity of the sweet shop.

"Hold our places," Sadie said. "I'll go scope out the choices." Myrtle nodded, and Sadie sidestepped the line, moving forward to look in the display cases. *Oh yes, this will do nicely!* She grinned, eagerly noting the wide variety of truffles, nut bars, caramel creations, thick slices of cake, and old-fashioned chocolate shakes. *Espresso meltaways, pecan turtles, maple nut creams, chocolate-covered cherries, amaretto truffles... how will we ever decide?*

"It's going to be a tough decision," Sadie said as she returned to Myrtle's side. "Too many options."

"That's a good problem to have," Myrtle pointed out. "We can take some back to the hotel. Did you see anything with caramel? I love caramel."

Sadie nodded. "Lots of it: with chocolate, without chocolate, with nuts, without nuts. Caramel in every shape and form."

Myrtle rubbed her hands together, a wicked smile on her face. "Perfect!"

As the line moved, they stepped forward little by little until they finally reached the counter. After enjoying a free sample and some quick debate—after all, there were customers behind them —they put together an enticing assortment to take with them, paid for the box of treats, and moved away from the counter.

"I believe a test is in order," Sadie said, veering toward a small table. She and Myrtle took seats in ice-cream-parlor-style chairs and opened the box, each choosing a sweet treat to try.

"Heaven," Myrtle exclaimed as she bit into a piece of chocolate caramel marble fudge.

"Poison," Sadie murmured, contemplating a cashew nut truffle suspiciously before quickly popping it into her mouth.

Myrtle choked on her caramel fudge. "What?" She glanced around. A woman at a nearby table was now eyeing her double chocolate milkshake with caution.

"Do you think it was poison?" Sadie said after finishing the truffle. "In the shrimp cocktail the director had before the show?"

Myrtle shrugged. "Who knows. It's one possibility, I guess. You think someone in the kitchen had it out for him?"

"Or someone who knew someone in the kitchen. Or had access to the food."

"Maybe a switch somewhere along the way in room service," Myrtle suggested. "Like someone in the show with a grudge. They could have intercepted the delivery to the room."

"Now you're thinking," Sadie said, impressed. "But who? That's the question."

Myrtle finished the caramel fudge and eyed the remaining chocolates, a decadent dozen or so. "How about we take this delicious stash of goodies back to the hotel and see if we can dig up some answers."

Sadie put the lid on the box and stood up. "Deal. Let's go."

EIGHT

The hum of activity in the casino buzzed at normal levels. If those intent on gambling were aware of the scenario that had unfolded in the main hotel and theater, they hadn't let it affect their concentration. Slot machine handles cranked up and down, dice tumbled across felt tabletops, and scantily clad servers delivered cocktails to waiting customers. A backdrop of calliope-type sounds soared through the air, set in flight by pinball machines.

Sadie surveyed the room, curious to see the casino operating like normal after the discovery of a dead body right in the same building. She found herself somewhat envious; concentration had never been her strong suit.

"Maybe they don't know," Myrtle said as if answering Sadie's unspoken question. Her eyes scanned the room as she shrugged her shoulders. "I would think at least the police would be in here."

"They're probably busy interviewing hotel and theater employees," Sadie said. "Interviewing casino patrons is probably not a top priority. I doubt someone is going to commit a murder and then go hang out at the craps table. They'll be long gone by now. I'd bet on that." Sadie chuckled at her use of words. There were plenty of bets going on around her, but it was unlikely any had to do with the killer's whereabouts.

"Or they could be hiding right here in plain sight," Myrtle suggested.

Sadie nodded. "Anything's possible, I suppose. You never know what might go on inside the mind of a criminal."

Myrtle tapped Sadie on the shoulder and nodded toward a pair of casino workers—as noted by matching vests and name tags—engaged in an intense conversation near a row of slot machines. The two employees, both attractive women, stood close to each other, and their frantic arm motions and quick head swivels implied more than a casual discussion. Myrtle leaned closer to Sadie. "Maybe they know something."

"They might," Sadie agreed. "They look distraught, so I'm sure they know what happened. Why don't you wander that way and see what you can overhear. I'll make the rounds."

"Maybe I can place a few bets while I'm investigating."

"Don't go too crazy," Sadie cautioned. "People can get into trouble when it comes to gambling."

Myrtle nodded, her expression serious. "I know. That's why I have a budget." She whipped a roll of nickels out of her purse and held it up proudly.

"I guess you're safe then," Sadie said. "You can't go too crazy."

"I won five dollars once at a little casino!" Myrtle beamed.

"Impressive. So you left with seven dollars?"

Myrtle tilted her head and thought about this. "No. Now that I think about it, I left with five. I guess it was a net win of three dollars. Still, I was able to buy one-fourth of a margarita with it!"

"Quite the jackpot." Sadie grinned.

"I thought so," Myrtle said. "I think I'll try for half a margarita this time." She set off in the direction of the slot machines, ostensibly stopping near the women arguing under the guise of checking her phone.

Sadie turned her attention to the center of the casino, taking stock of the activity as she wandered through the cavernous room. Some of the gaming tables sat empty while others hosted small groups or couples. A variety of expressions dotted customer faces, indicating optimism, frustration, and even boredom.

Of particular interest to her was a roulette table where several people stood by impatiently, presumably waiting for a dealer. The odd bunch included a red-headed woman with a bouffant hairdo and an elderly man wearing a polka-dot bow tie, among others.

Roulette had always seemed like a fun game to Sadie, what with the spinning wheel and all. But the real draw came when the two women who had been arguing on the side walked out to the playing area. Both appeared upset, especially one of particular interest to Sadie, the dealer who took a place at the blackjack table, not far from the roulette table. The statuesque woman had a slender build with seductively ample curves and a bright blue streak in her platinum hair. Remembering the conversation in the boutique dressing room, she felt certain this was the dealer with the special connection to the show director.

"Maybe we can get a roulette game in and watch the blackjack dealer at the same time? What do you think, Coco?" A tiny yip followed, which Sadie always took as agreement. It made decisions so much easier when the answer was always yes.

Sadie approached the roulette game while eyeing the nearby blackjack dealer who had picked up a deck of cards and was deftly shuffling them. This caused her to crash into the roulette table unexpectedly, much to the disapproval of both the roulette dealer and players. At least the wheel wasn't spinning, so a profuse apology seemed to pacify them, although the looks she received spoke of annoyance at best and disgust at worst.

"Would you like to join in?" the roulette dealer asked hesitantly. Sadie noted the diminutive brunette had striking green eyes that appeared swollen in spite of an obvious attempt to cover that up with makeup. Her name tag read BRANDI.

Sadie glanced over at the blackjack dealer, hoping to read the name tag on her uniform. But it was too small to be read from where she stood.

"Why not?" Sadie quipped enthusiastically as she turned back to Brandi, earning additional looks from those around the table, these even less friendly than before. *Tough crowd*, Sadie thought as she pondered the numbers and black and red markings on the wheel. Did she have a lucky number? She'd heard that 777 was lucky in gambling, yet there was no such number on the wheel, not even a 77. She decided to go with 7, rationalizing that she'd have at least a third of the luck that 777 would have given her. At least it was a theory.

Soon armed with a stack of blue chips—neither the dealer nor the woman who had already chosen pink chips seemed amused when Sadie proposed to switch colors—Sadie placed her bet on the number 7. "Our lucky number," she whispered to Coco, leaning toward her tote bag. She watched as others stacked chips on various numbers and lines. The dealer flicked a ball inside the outer circle of the roulette wheel, starting a lengthy spin in the opposite direction of the marked wheel itself. She waved her hand across the table, palm down, above the chips, announcing, "No more bets," as the wheel continued to spin.

Mesmerized by the swirling sound of the circling ball inside the wheel and intent on getting a better look at the blackjack dealer, Sadie leaned forward, oblivious to the fact her tote bag came to rest at an even height with the table. Only when the woman with the bouffant hairdo gasped did Sadie realize Coco had escaped and was in the process of hopscotching down the betting area, splaying chips left and right as she went along. The man with the bow tie tried to grab the petite Yorkie but was not quick enough. Coco bolted away, landing on the wheel itself, where she stood frozen, wide-eyed, as the wheel continued to spin.

"She never did like merry-go-rounds," Sadie said as she hustled to the wheel in an attempt to retrieve the wayward canine. She managed to convince Coco to come to her just as the swirling sound began to slow. As the Yorkie jumped off the wheel, one paw tapped the ball as it dropped, conveniently knocking it into the number seven spot.

"Well!" Sadie exclaimed to a stunned audience after scooping Coco into her arms. "Did we win?"

NINE

"So you got kicked out," Myrtle said, her tone both sympathetic and amused as she dropped into a chair across from Sadie.

Sadie had thanked the security guards profusely at the entrance to the lobby as if they'd done her a grand favor in accompanying her rather than simply making sure she left the casino floor. One had quirked an eyebrow; the other had mumbled a dispassionate "you're welcome." Clearly puzzled at Sadie's demeanor—perhaps others being thrown out of a casino didn't take it well—they'd returned to their posts, and Sadie had found her way to the coffee kiosk, ordering a macchiato with double whipped cream in order to justify occupying a table until Myrtle could join her.

Sadie huffed. "Let's just say I was escorted out."

"Firmly," Myrtle noted.

"Yes, indeed." Sadie bristled. "And I dare say that's no way to treat a guest over a little mishap."

"And what little mishap was that?"

"Coco decided she wanted to play roulette."

"Did she bet any money?"

"Well, no, come to think of it."

"That was likely the problem," Myrtle suggested. "Next time have her wager a treat or two."

"Somehow I'm not sure that would have made a difference." Sadie took a sip of her macchiato. "I think she might have enjoyed the ride on the roulette wheel, although she looked slightly terrified while on it. I think she was yipping to go back while we were…"

"Being thrown out?" Myrtle offered.

Sadie sighed. "Yes, I suppose that's the way it was. At least I got to observe the blackjack dealer who is—er, make that who *was*—somehow connected to the show director."

"Did you find anything out?"

"Not a darn thing except that she's quite the looker." And she was, Sadie had to admit—tall and slender but rather voluptuous with an odd countenance that said both cheap and elegant. "I couldn't get a grip on her personality from where I was at the roulette table. She certainly knows how to shuffle a deck of cards." *And maybe more*, Sadie thought to herself. *Like men, money, and possibly murder?*

Myrtle sighed. "Well, she does sound like she could attract attention from a ladies' man. Maybe the show director was that type."

"Josie made it sound like he was. We could ask if we run into her again," Sadie suggested. "I wonder if the cast will stay here or take a break until the show opening is rescheduled."

"If he was that type, there might have been some jealousy floating around," Myrtle suggested. "Maybe he was involved with several people and one of them decided to do something about it."

"You mean another lover, jealous enough to kill?"

Myrtle shrugged her shoulders. "It's possible. Or the blackjack dealer might have a jealous husband or boyfriend."

"That's another option," Sadie agreed. "Or this may have nothing to do with the dealer at all."

"True." Myrtle nodded. "Which leaves…?"

"All kinds of things." Sadie ran possibilities through her mind. "Maybe he was in debt. Maybe he was involved in something shady with the show finances. Or maybe this had nothing to do with the show at all."

"Maybe his death really was accidental," Myrtle suggested.

"With the police around and a detective telling us to stay out of it?" Sadie shook her head. "No, this was no accident."

"Don't forget about that shrimp cocktail," Myrtle said. "Someone could have tampered with it."

Sadie pondered this. "I'm sure they'll test it. And don't forget the room was already disturbed before that was delivered. The room service person said so. And if Seth was already dead, she would have reported that too, so he wasn't dead yet. The assistant director is the one who found him."

"Who would now be the actual director, right?"

"I would think so," Sadie said. "He'd be the logical one to take over."

"It sounds like we could use some inside information." Myrtle tapped her chin, her glittered manicure sparkling under the overhead lights of the lobby. "I wonder who we could get that from… Perhaps an officer from another precinct, another state even…"

Sadie shook her head, knowing exactly where Myrtle was headed. "I'm not bringing Broussard into this." Just the thought of telling her New Orleans detective-turned-beau that she'd fallen into another murder scenario was enough to keep her from calling him. Besides, they hadn't planned to be in touch during the girls weekend she and Myrtle had planned. This would allow a little more girl time without any male input or interference. Not that Broussard interfered with anything. The long-distance relationship suited them both just fine, in fact made it more romantic. Absence making the heart grow fonder and all that.

"It was just an idea," Myrtle said.

"Not a bad one," Sadie admitted. "But we were going to keep a 'no men allowed' status on this weekend."

Much to Sadie's amusement, Myrtle clucked softly and flapped her elbows away from her sides.

"I'm *not* chicken," Sadie countered, dismissing the implied accusation with a swish of her hand. "I could call him, and maybe I will. But I don't see that he could help. Besides, he'll tell me to back away from all this, and then I'll either have to lie or follow his advice, in which case we won't find anything out."

Myrtle let her elbows relax at her sides. "You have a point. And I'm too curious to let this drop."

"Did you find anything out from the casino dealers who were arguing?" Sadie immediately followed this with a second question. "Wait, first things first. Did you win anything?"

Myrtle beamed with pride. "Lost two dollars, won two dollars, lost two dollars, then won *five* dollars."

"Mighty impressive," Sadie observed with a grin. "Don't spend it..."

"...all in one place," Myrtle said, quickly finishing Sadie's predictable comment. "Besides, five dollars only goes so far."

"Um..." Sadie tapped her fingers on the edge of her macchiato cup. *Here we go again.* "You only won three dollars."

"No, I won five on the last round," Myrtle said.

"But you started with two, which you lost."

Myrtle shifted in her chair. "And won again."

"And lost again."

"Right," Myrtle said. "And then I won five."

Sadie sighed. Perhaps math was not Myrtle's strong suit. Though it was true she'd won five dollars, provided losing the two initial dollars didn't count. And who was counting anyway? This was just a vacation. At least it *was* just a vacation before the show's director kicked the bucket. Or perhaps had the bucket kicked *for* him.

"The question is who kicked that bucket..." Sadie mused.

"What bucket?" Myrtle raised a questioning eyebrow.

"The director's bucket," Sadie said, surprised to find she'd uttered the comment aloud. "Which brings me back to my original question before we got sidetracked into analyzing your slot machine high finances. What did you learn from the women?"

"Not a lot," Myrtle admitted. "They were whispering most of the time, plus they were emotional. And it was hard to hear over the dinging those machines make."

"You must have heard something," Sadie pressed. "Anything?"

"I heard the director's name mentioned more than once," Myrtle recalled. "They were definitely talking about him. One of them said, 'We should have known better,' and the other one said, 'I'm going to miss him.'"

"Which one said which?"

"I'm not sure," Myrtle said. "I couldn't see their faces. I didn't want to look up from my phone and, you know, break my cover!" She fought back a smile, presumably pleased with her turn of phrase.

"Well, that could mean something," Sadie said, also impressed with the detective-speak. *Should have known better about what?*

"I also heard a blackjack reference," Myrtle continued.

"Probably because one of them was the blackjack dealer the ladies in the dressing room mentioned," Sadie said. "The one that had the argument with the show director. That's how I ended up at the roulette table. Because it was close enough to the blackjack table to watch her."

"They must have more than one dealer," Myrtle pointed out. "Maybe that's not the one they were talking about."

Sadie nodded. "I'm sure they have others. But I recognized this one as soon as she walked out on the floor. She fits the description: 'a floozie with a blue streak in her platinum hair.'"

"That does sound fairly specific."

"If only I could get back in there to see her again."

"I don't recommend trying. At least not right away," Myrtle said. "Getting thrown out twice in the same day could be discouraging."

"Thanks for pointing that out." Sadie rolled her eyes. "Don't worry. I'll figure some way to get back in there."

Myrtle chuckled. "I'm sure you will."

TEN

Over coffee and chocolate croissants, Sadie and Myrtle discussed plans for the day. "Breakfast of champions!" Sadie had proclaimed when contemplating a quick morning pastry indulgence in lieu of the breakfast buffet.

"Shopping could be a good way to start the day," Sadie proposed.

Myrtle simply nodded, having just taken a bite of croissant.

"Or maybe... shopping," Sadie suggested. "Then again, shopping sounds appealing."

"I see what you're doing there. Though another spa indulgence would be nice," Myrtle said, now between bites. "I wonder if Tawny is working today. She seems to know the inside scoop on things. We could call down to the spa and find out."

"Good idea. Maybe she'd know what Brandi and Stacey meant by saying, 'we should have known better.'"

"Do you think they were talking about Seth?" Myrtle asked. "They could have been talking about anything."

Sadie finished her croissant and took a sip of her coffee, notably a mocha version. "They very well could have. You said they were both emotional."

"Absolutely," Myrtle said. "And don't forget one of them said 'I'm going to miss him.' I wonder what that means."

"I don't think it necessarily means anything," Sadie said.

"Doesn't that imply innocence? That they wouldn't have had anything to do with the murder?" Myrtle questioned.

"Not necessarily," Sadie said. "No one can be presumed innocent at first."

"What about 'innocent until proven guilty?'"

Sadie shook her head. "In a courtroom, yes. But if you immediately assume people are innocent when first investigating, it's easy to overlook details."

"Maybe you should have gone into law enforcement or private detective work," Myrtle said. "Officially I mean. You have a feel for it."

Sadie chuckled. "I'm quite certain owning a fashion boutique is more fun."

"Speaking of fun," Myrtle said, "look who's having a good time over there. They're not looking so emotional today."

Sadie followed Myrtle's subtle gesture, noticing Brandi and Stacey strolling through the lobby, whispering to each other and laughing.

"Curious," Sadie said.

"Indeed."

"It looks like they're heading out," Sadie said as she watched the two dealers head toward the exit. "I think I have a sudden urge to take a walk." She stood up.

"I feel the same urge," Myrtle said.

After disposing of their coffee cups and croissant wrappings, they headed for the front doors.

A cacophony of Las Vegas noise surrounded them the moment they exited the hotel. Tourists crowded the sidewalk, gawking at the extravagant facades of buildings designed to draw people inside, their wallets along with them. Water fountains danced across the street, coordinated with show tunes blasted over an outdoor sound system. Cars sat idling bumper to bumper on the boulevard. Impatient drivers honked as they waited for traffic to move along. Rap music boomed from one rolled-down window, at times drowning out the fountains' symphony while other times oddly keeping time with the music.

"There they are," Sadie said, pointing as she spotted Brandi and Stacey heading away from the hotel. "We can't lose them." Myrtle nodded, following Sadie close behind as she took off along the crowded sidewalk.

The two casino dealers moved along at a good clip, covering three blocks before pausing to look in a shop window. As they debated the window display, Sadie and Myrtle held back, taking the opportunity to catch their breath.

"Dang," Myrtle exclaimed as she leaned against a lamppost for support. "I'm not as young as I used to be. Have we only gone three blocks? Are you sure it's not three miles?"

Sadie propped herself against the other side of the lamppost, keeping an eye on the two women, still window shopping, at the same time. "Feels like three miles to me," she wheezed. "Maybe we should be hanging out in the fitness center instead of the spa." She glanced at Myrtle, who met her gaze. "Nah," they both said.

"They're on the move. Let's go." Sadie tapped Myrtle's arm, and they took off again. A few additional pauses later for more window shopping, Sadie and Myrtle saw the two women step beneath an archway and disappear into a crowd. They hurried to catch up with them, allowing several people to enter in front of them so as not to call attention to themselves. Others followed, and they soon found themselves in a congested line.

"Should we try to back out?" Myrtle glanced around, assessing the crowd.

Sadie eyed the line behind them. "We'll have to get a bunch of people to move. And we'll lose track of Brandi and Stacey if we leave. Let's hang in here." Myrtle nodded.

The line shuffled along and eventually reached a set of stairs. Excited voices floated down to them as they climbed higher. Now intrigued, Sadie and Myrtle followed along until the flooring leveled out and they could once again see the two women ahead.

"What are those kids next to them doing?" Myrtle said. "They're attaching some sort of... harnesses. Is that what those are? Is this line we're in for... zip-lining?" She looked at Sadie, eyes wide.

"No!" Sadie shouted. She lowered her voice as heads turned, and she leaned toward Myrtle. "It can't be! We would have seen a sign."

"We weren't looking at signs!" Myrtle pointed out. "We were just focused on following them! There must have been a sign back at that archway."

Sadie gulped. She'd never been fond of heights, and the combination of height and motion was nothing less than terrifying. She looked behind her again, hoping for an escape route. But the enthusiastic crowd was even more compact than it had been earlier.

"I only see one way out of this," Sadie said.

Myrtle debated the crowd. "Is this where the expression 'the only way out of some things is through them' comes from?"

"Undoubtedly first spoken by someone trapped in a zip-lining queue." Sadie took a deep breath, zipped her tote bag tightly closed, and hugged it against her side. A muffled yip followed. She watched as Brandi and Stacey stepped off the platform and more people lined up for harnesses. Soon they were next in line. They waited as those people headed out and then took their places.

"First time, ladies?" a young man barely—if even—out of his teens grinned as he and a partner of similar age helped Sadie and Myrtle into harnesses.

"Hardly!" Myrtle exclaimed. "We do this all the time!" She looked at Sadie, eyes even wider than before. Sadie mirrored her expression.

"Is that so?" The second of the young men smirked but not unkindly. He tested straps and clips on Sadie's harness while the other worker inspected Myrtle's.

Sadie double-checked that her tote bag was closed, relieved to find it fit securely inside her safety harness.

"Let's make sure your bag is safe." The young man adjusted the strap until both the strap and bag were secure. "You wouldn't want to lose anything in that tote of yours."

"You have no idea," Sadie said as she and Myrtle exchanged nervous glances.

"You'll be fine, ladies." He and the other employee exchanged glances, which Sadie took as either a good sign or a very, very bad sign. "Go ahead and step forward. Place your feet on the lines there on the edge of the platform."

Myrtle took one last look at Sadie. "Well, we did say we'd follow them."

"That we did," Sadie said, trying not to glance down. "But this might just be beyond the call of duty."

"Ready?" one of the young men asked.

"No!" both Sadie and Myrtle yelled just before grinning at each other and stepping forward.

ELEVEN

"I certainly wasn't expecting that adventure," Myrtle said as she tossed off her shoes and rubbed her feet.

"That makes two of us!" Sadie dropped into a corner chair, sagging against the plush backing. She lifted Coco out of the tote bag and placed her on the floor, where the pup could run free. She then dropped her head back on the top of the chair and gazed at the ceiling. The unexpected zip ride had been an ordeal, both from a physical and emotional aspect. It had been all she could do to not turn and flee at the last minute. But Myrtle had been ready to launch, and she knew it wouldn't have been fair to desert her, regardless of how scared she felt. Besides, challenges were good for building character, right?

"I'm going to need a nap before dinner." Myrtle flopped down on the bed. "I need time for my stamina to catch up with my appetite."

Sadie nodded as she gave Coco a pat on the head. A nap did sound appealing.

"Let's meet up in about an hour and a half," Myrtle suggested. "What about hitting the buffet again?"

"Sounds perfect to me. Good chance to overhear some

conversations." Any area conducive to eavesdropping seemed like a good choice.

Sadie called Coco, and the two of them retreated to their own room in order to give Myrtle time for her nap. Sadie, however, although physically tired, found herself too keyed up to rest. She helped herself to a beverage from the honor bar and curled up in a chair. Coco jumped into her lap.

"I'm sorry to have put you through that," Sadie said as she stroked the pup's fuzzy head. "Zipping you inside the bag and everything." Coco responded with a sweet look that Sadie thought held just a touch of reprimand. "We're all safe, though, and that's what counts. And it wasn't all that bad after the jumping-off part. In fact, it was sort of fun, don't you think? Almost like flying!" Coco emitted a Yorkie-sized huff, and Sadie knew the pup didn't share her enthusiasm. Coco had never been fond of being zippered in. A type of canine claustrophobia, she surmised.

Debating how to pass the time while Myrtle was napping, Sadie decided to shower and dress for dinner, seeing as she couldn't seem to relax. She set her drink aside, lowered Coco to the floor, and proceeded to rummage through the closet in search of something to wear. The hotel buffet was hardly a formal setting, but being on vacation always brought a certain mood with it that said "dress for fun." She laid out a flouncy, multicolored, floral skirt and a bright yellow boatneck tunic. Complementing these with a strand of red Venetian skunk beads—she loved that the little dots on them reminded her of dice—and shiny red flats, she showered, dressed, spiffed up her hair and makeup, and slid a note under Myrtle's door, saying she'd meet her at the buffet later.

The lobby was a hubbub of activity when she stepped out of the elevator. A long line snaked out from the registration counter as guests waited to check in. The coffee cart was equally busy. Enthusiastic noise from the casino carried into the lobby. She would have welcomed a chance to snoop around again or even to hit the slot machines to see if she could match Myrtle's supposed good fortune with them. But Sadie's better judgment told her it was too soon for another visit, especially in view of Coco's newfound love of roulette.

Settling on a self-guided tour of the hotel, she headed for the gift shop, surprised she hadn't already checked it out. It was often the first place she popped into when traveling. Somehow she'd been too distracted to do so this time. It seemed casino mix-ups, canceled productions, and little details like a dead body tended to upend regular routines. But she never missed a chance to peruse the goods in a hotel gift shop, so she headed for the door beneath the Art Deco-style sign welcoming customers to ALL THAT JAZZ.

Sadie considered herself a connoisseur of gift shops in general, having visited dozens—okay, admittedly hundreds—of them during her lifetime. She'd found the most remarkable souvenirs in them over the years, and this one looked promising. It was larger than many, which was always a plus, and divided into organized sections according to merchandise: clothing here, jewelry there, books and paper goods over yonder, snacks and drinks in yet another section.

"Where should we begin?" As was her habit, she said this aloud, directing the question to her tote bag, although not expecting a response.

"How about over there?" a voice answered, causing Sadie to look around, her gaze landing on a young girl behind a sales counter. Sadie estimated her to be barely twenty if even that. She had her arm held out in a gesture toward the clothing section. Sadie guessed the bright outfit she'd pulled out of her closet hinted at her love for clothing.

"An excellent suggestion!" Sadie replied, immediately spying a purple silk scarf that would nicely complement a pair of grape cluster earrings she'd picked up on a wine country outing. She took the scarf to the counter, along with an identical one in bright peach, and continued to browse. Not surprisingly, she noticed copies of *The Great Gatsby* among a book display. She picked up a copy and held it up to the girl at the counter.

"We read that in school," the girl said. "It was pretty good, I guess."

"Yes, I read it in school too," Sadie agreed. "But not quite as recently as you, I imagine." She grinned, and to the girl's credit, she grinned as well. "Wouldn't hurt to read it again, get in the spirit of things here." She added it to the counter with the scarves.

A voice just behind her startled Sadie, having not heard footsteps approaching over the Scott Joplin music playing over the shop sound system.

"Can I get my package that's on hold?"

Sadie was tempted to correct "can" to "may" and suggest adding a "please" to the request, but a quick sideways glance told her the new arrival at the counter was Brandi. She had no desire to tangle with the roulette dealer again. Hoping to not be recognized, she turned away, thinking to browse a rack of rhinestone sweatshirts with the Speakeasy logo. But she was soon called back.

"Aren't you that guest with the rascally dog?"

Sadie was relieved to see the young woman smiling, her tone of voice friendly rather than reprimanding.

"Guilty as charged," Sadie said.

"I hope you know I didn't choose to throw you out," Brandi said. "That was Dylan's call, and security follows whatever he says."

"Dylan?" Sadie said, not recognizing the name.

"The floor manager," Brandi said. "I would have let you stay. I thought it was funny, and your little dog is so cute. What's its name?"

"Her name is Coco." Predictably, this was followed by a yip from Sadie's tote bag upon Coco hearing her name.

"Oh, of course!" Brandi chirped. "She's with you! Can I say hello?"

Can and may, Sadie thought again as she opened the tote and, looking around, lifted the sweet Yorkie out.

"Hi Coco," Brandi cooed as she gave the pup's head a pat. "You're so cute! And your sparkly pink rhinestone collar is precious!" She looked at Sadie and sighed. "I'd love to have a dog. My work hours are just all over the place. It wouldn't be fair. And Dylan doesn't like dogs anyway."

"Dylan, the floor manager?"

"Oh right," Brandi said, realizing information was missing from the conversation. "Yes, the same Dylan who's the floor manager. He also happens to be my boyfriend."

"Ah, got it," Sadie said. "Well, it must be nice to work together. Maybe?"

Brandi rolled her eyes. "I don't know about that. The past couple of months he's been stressed, especially at work." She gave Coco another scrunch on the head and turned back to the counter for her package. Thanking the girl at the counter for holding her purchase, she said a quick goodbye to Sadie, added an extra goodbye to Coco, and headed back out.

"That was interesting," Sadie whispered to Coco as she set her back in the tote, getting a yip of agreement in return. She browsed the shop's offerings a few more minutes, selected a third color of the scarf—she firmly believed you could never have too many color choices of the same item—paid for her purchases, and left.

Twelve

Sadie stepped into Gatsby's Grill and looked around, spotting Myrtle waving both arms in the air from a table not far from the baked-potato bar. Sadie hurried across the room and plopped into the chair across from her friend.

"Sticking close to the carbs, I see," Sadie said, noting a tower of foil-wrapped potatoes.

"You know it," Myrtle replied, glancing at the serving area. "But..." She turned back to face Sadie. "I was debating a baked potato with a gazillion toppings, but I think I'm going to get my carb intake at the pasta bar tonight. They've got four different pastas and three choices for sauce. And lasagna. And garlic cheesy bread."

Sadie nodded. "I've never been one to turn down Italian food. Though tonight..." She thought back to the selections the buffet had when they were there before. "I might just start with a big salad."

Myrtle frowned. "I'm all for salad and healthy eating, but is that all you're going to have?"

"Heavens no!" Sadie exclaimed as if Myrtle had just suggested something unimaginable. It was an all-you-can-eat buffet, of course, and they were on vacation. "I fully intend to visit the dessert bar! It would be terrible not to try a few of those that I missed last time. And they do cancel each other out, you know."

"The salad and the dessert?"

"Absolutely!" Sadie grinned. "Maybe even enough to throw in some fried zucchini in between."

"That's the spirit," Myrtle said, rising from her chair. Sadie followed, keeping her tote bag close to her side.

Pleased to find the lines weren't terribly long, they split up, gathered their food choices, and met back at the table. A server had dropped off glasses of water, silverware, and napkins while they were away.

"Quite a salad you have there," Myrtle noted. She looked down at her own plate of fettuccini as if questioning her choice and then looked back up, taking inventory of Sadie's plate with remarkable detail. "Lettuce, tomatoes, cucumber, olives, cheese, slivered almonds, shredded chicken, black beans, corn, dried cranberries, marinated mushrooms, carrots, avocado, and... sheesh, who knows what else you have in there? I have to admit the french fries on top are a nice touch."

Sadie nodded as she dropped a fry into her tote bag, resulting in a yip of delight. "Always nice to switch things up. That's my philosophy."

"More fun than croutons, right?"

"Oh, don't worry, those are in there too," Sadie said nonchalantly. She lifted a ramekin of ranch dressing off one side of the salad plate, poured a hearty portion on the salad, and set the rest aside for dipping, which she immediately tested with a fry.

"Quite a crowd here tonight." Myrtle twirled some pasta onto her fork, took a bite, and looked around.

"Well, best bang for your buck, I think, don't you?" Sadie contemplated her mountain of salad, considering she might have gone a touch overboard. She held her fork off to the side, unsure where she could take a stab without it overflowing.

"Psst, Sadie, look," Myrtle whispered.

"Why are we whispering?" Sadie leaned forward and whispered, "This place is a zoo. No one can hear you. I can barely hear you myself." She sat back, stabbed a cherry tomato with her fork, and popped it into her mouth.

"Look! Way over in that corner." Myrtle tilted her head sharply several times in one direction in an attempt to avoid pointing.

"You're going to get a kink in your neck if you keep that up," Sadie cautioned.

"That's the guy who gave me the tickets in the elevator that first night. But that's *not* the woman he was with then."

Sadie dipped another fry in the ranch dressing and followed Myrtle's gaze to a booth in a poorly lit corner of the restaurant. "He doesn't look familiar to me." She looked more carefully and raised an eyebrow. "But I can tell you who the woman is. That's Stacey, the blackjack dealer from the casino."

"You're right!" Myrtle exclaimed. "I didn't pay attention to the dealers when we were in the casino, since I only played the slots. But I recognize her from that zip-lining adventure you made me go on."

"Hey, that wasn't my idea!"

"Well, it wasn't mine either," Myrtle pointed out. "But it was kind of exciting."

Sadie set her fork down and focused her attention on the couple in the corner. Their positioning and body language gave the appearance of a clandestine meeting made to not look clandestine. Like an affair hidden out in the open or at least some kind of less-than-forthcoming exchange.

"Remind me what the lady in the elevator was like." Sadie kept an eye on the corner table while waiting for Myrtle's answer, which was on hold at the moment for fettuccine. Myrtle waved one finger in the air to indicate a reply was forthcoming.

Myrtle swallowed and shrugged. "I only saw her for sixty seconds or so, and I wasn't paying attention until that guy shoved the tickets in my hands."

"You said she acted upset when he gave you the tickets, right?"

Myrtle nodded. "Very upset. She definitely didn't know he was going to."

"Because they were expensive? Because she wanted to see the show? To have a night out on the town?"

"Maybe all of the above," Myrtle said. "She seemed stunned when he handed them to me. I have to admit, it felt like a very impulsive move on his part. I don't think he was planning to give them away. It was almost like he panicked. In any case, she became very agitated."

"Well, maybe that"—Sadie tilted her head in the direction of the couple—"has something to do with it."

"Maybe. They do look rather cozy." Myrtle pushed her plate to the side and took a sip of water. "Look, they're leaving. Or maybe only he's leaving."

Sadie glanced over and watched the man walk out. "I know this drill, Myrtle. Give her two minutes and she'll walk out too." She set her salad plate aside and waited. Sure enough, with only a calculated pause after the man exited, Stacey also left.

"You sure called that one," Myrtle said.

"It looked pretty obvious to me." Sadie stood and set her napkin on the table. "But I'm still not sure what was going on over there." She eyed the empty booth as if there might be a remaining clue.

"Maybe a little sugar infusion will help us figure out what we just saw," Myrtle suggested, also standing.

"It's worth a try." Sadie slung her tote bag over her shoulder and followed Myrtle to the dessert area. "Maybe several tries," she added as she looked over the selections.

"Oh my!" Myrtle exclaimed. "This is impossible. Look at those chocolate truffles... and the strawberry cheesecake... and the mini key lime pies... and, wow, I don't know where to start."

"If you go for the minis, you'll be able to try more things," Sadie suggested.

"Excellent point." Myrtle grabbed a small plate from a stack at the end of the bar and proceeded to choose several items. Sadie followed suit, leaning toward the chocolate side, as always, but managed to get a bite-sized lemon bar and mini apple pie in the mix. The two returned to their seats, finding their server had removed their dinner plates and tidied up the table. They set their dessert choices down and wasted no time digging in.

"Vacation, so no calories, right?" Myrtle said.

"Absolutely." Sadie grinned. "Besides, we can work it off shopping. I'd like to go back to that Las Vegas Lily's shop."

"I'm up for a shopping trip tomorrow." Myrtle took a bite of a salted caramel blondie, closed her eyes, and sighed.

Sadie dipped her fork into a serving of a s'mores trifle, her reaction matching Myrtle's. "Why did I go to the salad bar first? I would have had more room for dessert if I hadn't."

"I think that was the point, Sadie."

"Of course. You're right." Sadie contemplated her assortment of mini desserts and came to a decision. "Myrtle, I think a walk after dinner would be a good idea. Work some of this off."

"I'm up for a good walk tonight."

Sadie nodded. "Perfect. Let's go."

Thirteen

A quick stop back to their rooms let Sadie and Myrtle grab sweaters for the evening walk. Although the warm Las Vegas weather indicated they probably wouldn't need anything, they both felt it was best to be prepared. Sadie grabbed a lightweight beige sweater that her San Francisco shop had carried the previous spring. Not surprisingly, most of her favorite clothes were from her own shop. This was not only because she brought them in wholesale, though getting everything at a discount was certainly a perk. But because she did ninety percent of the buying. She ordered clothes that she loved herself, adding a few other things that caught her eye because she knew her customers' tastes.

Sweater in hand, she met up with Myrtle in her room, who had a shawl of sorts draped over her arm. Their timing for the quick room stopover turned out to be fortuitous, as the atrium light show they'd yet to see flashed its first laser beam as they were getting ready to leave the room. Accordingly, they rushed to the window and looked down to the garden area below. Situated in one corner, a red rock formation set the base for red, blue, purple, and green flashing lights that shot upward. Three side-by-side fountains launched undulating bursts of water, and when they died down, a screen appeared with an old-time silent film show-ing. Guests and visitors roaming the atrium took seats at benches to watch the film.

"How unusual," Sadie said. "What a bizarre mix of lights, fountains, and film, all set into a red rock background."

"And now there's a movie?" Myrtle pressed her head against the window, trying to get a better look.

Sadie followed Myrtle and pressed her forehead against the window. "I read somewhere that many silent films were only a few minutes long with some around fifteen minutes," Sadie said. "So this works for a show finale. Pretty clever, really. And, oh! There's Detective Tanner!"

"Where?"

"On the screen!"

Myrtle stepped back and playfully smacked Sadie's arm. "That's Charlie Chaplin and you know it."

Sadie laughed, tossed her sweater around her shoulders, and started for the door. "Let's go."

Sadie and Myrtle stepped out of the hotel and looked around. The sidewalk was just as crowded as it had been in the daytime. It had a different energy to it, a sort of buzz that Sadie couldn't quite put her finger on. But it was invigorating, and she was delighted they'd decided to venture out.

"Now this is the type of Las Vegas night that I love," Sadie said. "I'm not much of a fan of gambling, and I can only take so much time in a bar."

"Unless the music is great, of course," Myrtle pointed out.

"Well, yes," Sadie agreed. "That does make a difference. I love the old-time jazz they play here at the Blind Pig: Al Jolson, Louis Armstrong, Bessie Smith. There are so many greats from that time period." She pulled her phone from a side pocket of her tote bag and aimed it at a particularly bright neon martini glass with an olive in it. "The lights at night here on the Strip? I never get tired of them." After taking several pictures, she slipped it back in the bag and gave Coco a scrunch on the head.

Myrtle looked up, marveling at the array of signs: elaborate hotel logos, flashing arrows at casino entrances, and the word *Vegas* scattered throughout. "They're just gorgeous, and they're everywhere you look. I love all the bright colors and glitz: fuchsia, turquoise, emerald, gold, and more. And so many of them are sparkling, twinkling like Christmas lights. They remind me of something... jewelry! That's what. I'd love to reach up and grab a couple of bright strings of lights and wear them for the evening. Wouldn't that be fun?"

"I never thought of it that way," Sadie said. "But I can see what you mean. Sort of like glow-in-the-dark jewelry." She and Myrtle exchanged glances. "Are you thinking what I'm thinking?"

Myrtle nodded. "We just might have to find some. Let's head for a souvenir shop. They'll have all kinds of odds and ends."

"What did you think about seeing the twosome in Gatsby's Grill tonight?" Sadie asked Myrtle as they strolled along the sidewalk.

"A little peculiar," Myrtle admitted.

"Like they were together but trying not to look like they were. You're sure that's the man who gave you the tickets?"

"Definitely. And I'm just as sure Stacey was *not* the woman he was with in the elevator. I'd remember that blue streak in her hair."

"Maybe a clandestine affair," Sadie said. "That's what it looked like."

Myrtle harrumphed. "Not all that clandestine if they're meeting in the hotel buffet. So maybe it wasn't that at all."

"Maybe." Sadie tapped Myrtle's arm and pointed to a souvenir shop. The two of them veered in that direction and soon found themselves surrounded by racks and shelves and counters and baskets and wooden trays and every sort of container imaginable, all filled with a crazy variety of knickknacks.

"Look at these," Myrtle said, holding up a pair of socks with a Las Vegas sign print. And they come in all these colors!" She ran her fingers across a row of socks.

"Multiple colors is always a plus in my book," Sadie said. "And look at this!" She shook a snow globe and watched poker chips float around amid glitter inside.

"I loved those when I was a little girl," Myrtle said, eyeing the snow globe. "I had one with a little cottage inside, something you might find in an English countryside. There was something magical about it as if just watching it was going on a vacation."

Myrtle moved to another display and picked up a tie with a roulette wheel design. "Now if only you could have this in a dog leash." Sadie eyed the tie and laughed. "That would be perfect, a little reminder of her shenanigans in the casino. But look over there." She pointed to a display of pet accessories and hustled over to it, Myrtle following.

"A Viva Las Vegas dog collar that lights up!" Sadie exclaimed. She dangled it over her tote, hoping she wouldn't appear to be shoplifting. Two yips followed, a general sign of approval—so she believed—from Coco. "We definitely need this."

Myrtle nodded. "Very cute. Just her style."

"And look!" Sadie said, waving Myrtle over to another rack. "Glow necklaces. Just what we were looking for."

"No bracelets?"

Sadie perused the rack. "No, but I bet you could circle this around your wrist more than once and make it a bracelet."

"In that case, I want two." Myrtle reconsidered this. "No, four. Er, maybe six."

"What color?"

"All different colors." Myrtle picked her choices off the display.

"Ditto." Sadie chose the ones that looked like they had the potential to be brightest, and both women made their purchases at the register.

"Now what?" Myrtle said once they'd stepped outside.

"Snap them so they begin to glow. Sadie activated the glow-in-the-dark jewelry and arranged them around her neck and wrists.

"Oh!" Sadie said as she and Myrtle continued on their walk. "I forgot to tell you who I bumped into at the gift shop earlier today."

"You went to a gift shop without me?" Myrtle chided.

"Just the hotel gift shop. You were napping."

"Ah, then you're forgiven." Myrtle reached in front of her and shook her arm to watch the makeshift glowing bracelets shake in the dark. "So, who did you see?"

"Brandi."

"Really?" Myrtle's eyes widened. "And did you get a lecture for disrupting the game? Or should I say having someone else disrupt the game?" She glanced at Sadie's tote bag.

"Not at all. In fact, she was friendly and even thought Coco's escapade was cute. Not that she could say so at the time. By the way, that floor manager, Dylan, is her boyfriend."

"Huh," Myrtle mused. "Seems like there's a casino cast that rivals the drama of the show."

"Which makes me wonder..." Sadie stopped under a particularly green neon light that added a paranormal glow to her face. "...what kind of connections there might be between the theater and the casino."

"I'm sure there's some crossover between them," Myrtle said as they continued walking. "How could there not be? They all work in the same building. There's bound to be some interaction."

Sadie nodded. "And many of them seem to hang out at the Blind Pig, which makes sense. It's convenient for them. I wonder if the show director was involved recently with anyone in the casino."

"Like the dealers?" Myrtle asked. "Well, Brandi just told you she's seeing Dylan, right?"

"Yes, but that doesn't mean she's been seeing him very long. We should ask Josie the next time we see her."

"I bet Brandi might be willing to talk too. Especially since she's fond of your assistant." Myrtle nodded toward Sadie's tote bag.

"That's a very good point," Sadie said, patting the side of her tote bag. "Coco has turned out to be an excellent assistant in the past. I suspect she's up for the challenge again. It's worth a try. Let's head back to the hotel."

Fourteen

Gatsby's Grill was relatively quiet when Sadie and Myrtle rolled in for breakfast. In fact, the overall hotel atmosphere was notably different from the evening energy. The music volume was lower, the lights were brighter, and the overall result was peaceful. Departing guests rolled luggage toward the registration counter to check out, and housekeeping employees were busy touching up lobby areas by dusting or sweeping. The playtime ambiance of the night was replaced with that of a new day beginning.

"It's certainly calm in here," Sadie pointed out as she looked around the buffet. "No waiting for a table." The room was half empty, a nice surprise after the dinner crowd.

"No doubt late-night casino guests and bar patrons are sleeping off their evening activities," Myrtle said. "The bar was certainly hopping last night."

"Let's sit over there," Sadie said, pointing to a booth against the wall. While a little distance from the buffet itself, it looked like a cozy place to start the day. They were soon seated, and an especially chipper server welcomed them. The young woman—barely out of her teens in Sadie's estimation, though it seemed everyone looked young to her these days—poured coffee and told them to help themselves to the breakfast offerings.

As was to be expected, the morning buffet setup was different than for later meals. Sadie, having splurged on the dessert bar the night before, was pleased to see platters of fresh honeydew melon, strawberries, and pineapple. These called to her immediately, and she helped herself to a nice variety. She looked longingly at a waffle that Myrtle chose—butter, syrup, and blueberry compote included—but opted for an omelet that was made on the spot by a chef. Keeping it simple with just cheese, mushrooms, and tomatoes, she helped herself to a glass of orange juice and returned to their table with her selections.

"Look over there," Myrtle said. She nodded across the room as she waved a fork full of waffle around in the air. "It's Josie. And she doesn't look very happy."

Sadie followed Myrtle's direction. Josie stood by a table where a man sat, attempting to eat his breakfast. Her body language was tense, and her arms gestured in such a way as to imply the conversation wasn't pleasant. From his facial expressions and the way he was attacking his food with his fork, Josie didn't seem to be the only one who was unhappy.

"You're right," Sadie said. "She definitely looks upset. I'd say they both look upset."

"Who do you think that is?" Myrtle squinted as if that would give her a better idea. "I don't recognize him."

"I don't know." Sadie racked her memory. "I don't think we've seen him before. I usually remember people."

"He doesn't look familiar." Myrtle took another bite of her waffle. "Maybe he's part of the show? Or a boyfriend? Ex-boyfriend? Husband?" She shrugged. "It could be anyone."

"I'm curious. Maybe she'll tell us," Sadie suggested. "At least she might tell us who he is, if he's with the show or not. Maybe we can get her attention after she finishes with him. Which I think she's doing now." Sadie waited for Josie to walk away from the man's table and then waved her over as she was about to pass their table.

"Good morning. Is everything okay?" Sadie said as Josie approached. She knew she was being pushy, but they'd formed somewhat of a friendship since they first met.

Josie swished her hand in a dismissive gesture. "Yeah, it's no big deal. Just Asher being a jerk, that's all. Hardly a news flash. Now that he's moved into the director position, he's going to be impossible. Nothing we say will matter. It'll be Asher's way or the highway, as they say."

"That's the assistant director from the show?" Sadie asked. "I mean, *was* the assistant director? And now he *is* the director? Isn't he the one who found... the director?"

Josie nodded. "Yeah, the stage manager sent him to Seth's room to see why he was late to the show."

"That must have been a horrible shock." Sadie shuddered and then took a sip of orange juice. "He sure jumped into that director role quickly, didn't he?"

"He didn't have a choice, not that it bothered him one bit, egomaniac that he is," Josie said. "The producers want the show going up as soon as possible. He knows the production better than anyone, so it only makes sense for him to take over. They're pushing him to pull everything together." She glanced around the room, seemingly nervous, and then leaned toward Sadie, lowering her voice. "Have you found anything out yet? About who might have killed Seth?"

Sadie shook her head. "Nothing yet. It's certainly intriguing." *Possibly more intriguing by the minute.*

"Well, keep me posted. I'll feel relieved when they figure out who did it," Josie said, her gaze still scanning the room before returning to Sadie and Myrtle. "They plan to open the show day after tomorrow. Will you still be here? I'd love for you to see it."

Sadie and Myrtle exchanged glances and nodded.

"I bet we can extend our stay," Sadie replied when she turned back to Josie. "I'll check with the front desk."

"Great. I think you'll enjoy it." Josie looked back at the new director and frowned.

Sadie looked around and saw Detective Tanner near the entrance. He spotted her, pointed to his eyes, then pointed to Sadie. She cheerfully waved back and pointed to the buffet with a thumbs-up.

Josie swept her arms to one side as if escorting a crowd into the theater. "You know what they say: The show must go on. There's money to be made. People have tickets. The big shots in finance aren't going to let that opportunity pass by. Honestly, I'll be glad to get back to work. We're rehearsing this afternoon. You two should come watch if you want."

Sadie perked up. "Rehearsals are open?"

Josie shook her head. "Not technically. But I can get you in. Asher is so overjoyed with his lofty new director status that he won't care."

"I guess enthusiasm is good when you're trying to rally people together after a shock," Myrtle said.

"I suppose so," Josie agreed. "It just seems he could show a little more restraint when Seth's death is so new. But his showbiz ego knows no bounds."

Sadie thought this over. "Why *is* he so enthusiastic?"

Josie laughed. "I'm sure he's over the moon about inheriting the director position. He's always had his eye on it but had to settle for assistant. He and Seth had a terrible fight over it, not that either of them really had a say in it. The producers wanted Seth from the start. He'd been included in several finance meetings even before the director position was filled."

"How frustrating for anyone else wanting the position," Sadie said.

"Asher also disagreed with most of Seth's decisions regarding the show," Josie continued, "always spouting off about how he would do things differently, even in front of everyone. He constantly tried to undermine him."

"That must have upset Seth even more," Myrtle said.

"That's an understatement!" Josie rolled her eyes. "They fought constantly whenever they were in the theater. You should have heard the fight they had at the final dress rehearsal! I was certain they were about to come to blows right there in front of the whole cast and crew."

"Did they?" Myrtle asked. "Come to blows?"

Josie shook her head. "No, but it was close."

"What about outside the theater?" Sadie asked. "Did that animosity carry over into their personal lives?"

Josie shrugged. "Who knows? I only saw them at rehearsals. From the way they clashed, I seriously doubt they could have been friends. They were probably glad to get out of each other's sight. *We* were all sure glad to get out of their sight too."

"Sounds understandable," Sadie said.

"In any case, come by the rehearsal today if you want. We start at noon. The door to the far left of the theater should be unlocked. It always is." Josie headed for the exit, glancing one last time at the new director's table.

"Well," Sadie said. "That was interesting. I dare say enlightening even."

"How do you figure?"

Sadie glanced at the man, quickly looking away before he caught her looking. "It sounds like the assistant director was very eager to be the director, rather desperate even. Which makes one wonder..."

"Wonder what?"

"Just exactly how desperate he was."

Fifteen

Sadie tried the door at the left of the theater, finding it open just as Josie had said it would be. She and Myrtle headed halfway down the aisle and took seats on the side where they wouldn't be too obvious. Although Josie had assured them it would be fine to observe the rehearsal, the new director's temperament seemed uncertain. They decided to play it safe and keep a low profile.

The stage was filled with activity. Dancers, Josie included, stretched in preparation for their numbers. Two stagehands eyed the floor, a clipboard in one hand and a roll of tape in the other. They stopped periodically to add tape to a location.

"Blocking," Myrtle whispered. "My college drama teacher always did this so we'd know where to stand."

"I didn't know you studied drama in college," Sadie said.

"Oh yes, indeed I did. And I loved every minute of it." Myrtle looked at the stage with an expression Sadie interpreted as wistful.

"You didn't want to pursue acting after college?"

Myrtle shook her head. "I thought about it, but I didn't have that kind of dedication. College shows were fun, and I even did a little community theater after that. But to try to make a career of it? With the politics and rejection and pressure? No, that wasn't for me."

A loudspeaker crackled and stopped, followed by music that started and stopped, followed yet again with a voice. "Testing, testing." Sadie cringed at a sudden squeal of feedback.

A familiar figure wearing a headset crossed the stage, one finger pressed against his ear.

"That's the guy who made that announcement the other night," Myrtle said. "When the show got canceled."

"The stage manager," Sadie confirmed. "What a terrible announcement to have to make. Remember how shaky he seemed? Understandable, of course. He would have just found out."

A sharp clap of hands brought their attention back to the stage as a man crossed in front of the performers and crew. Even from their vantage point halfway back in the theater, Sadie and Myrtle could sense the air of importance—or rather, self-importance—the man projected. Those he addressed looked attentive but not especially enthusiastic. Several dancers continued to stretch. One of the stagehands marked another spot in the floor while the other slid the roll of tape onto his wrist like a bracelet.

"We've all had a terrible shock, losing Seth so unexpectedly," the man began in a tone Sadie thought was somewhat too cheerful for the circumstances. "But we have a show to put on and not a minute to waste. It's time for us all to keep a *stiff upper lip*." He piped out "stiff upper lip" with a fake British accent that made not only Sadie and Myrtle cringe but at least half the cast on the stage. Someone in the wings coughed, and one dancer adjusted a leg warmer in an attempt—Sadie suspected—to hide a smile.

"That's Asher, the new director," Sadie said. "That's who Josie was talking to in the buffet."

"He does seem to think he's something special," Myrtle said. "Look at the way he struts around the stage."

"Yes," Sadie agreed. "And from the looks on the performers' faces, he thinks he's far more special than they think he is."

After numerous commands and a flamboyant pep talk that was met with reserved expressions and more than one roll of the eyes, Asher left the stage via side stairs, sat in the front row, and shouted a command to get started. The lights dimmed and the music cued up—without feedback, much to Sadie's relief—and the rehearsal began. Although broken up with repeated stops by Asher, during which he shouted a wide variety of corrections and no compliments, Sadie and Myrtle found it fascinating. It was clear it would be a good show once seen as a full production with costumes and without stops and restarts.

"I love those dance numbers," Sadie exclaimed. "The music from that time period is so catchy."

"I'm glad our tickets are being honored for the new opening date," Myrtle said.

"Maybe that's because they were VIP seats," Sadie offered. "Otherwise, they already had tickets sold. I imagine they had to refund most from the other night." Sadie noticed Myrtle's head looking around her, and she turned to see what had caught her attention.

"There's that guy." Myrtle pointed to the back corner of the theater. "The one we saw with Stacey in the buffet."

Sadie followed her gaze, noting a man in the last row, against the theater wall, a cell phone up to his ear. "He must be heavily involved with the show to be sitting in for rehearsal. He's probably trying to make sure the investment pays off."

"Maybe," Myrtle agreed. "I wonder if Josie would know."

"Let's find out." Sadie stood up and grabbed her tote bag. "Maybe we can get backstage and talk to her. It's worth a try."

"Out through the hallway again?" Myrtle raised an eyebrow.

Sadie shook her head. "I don't think that's necessary this time." She pointed to a door near the stage. "Let's try this way. I'm sure that door leads backstage."

Glancing one last time at the far corner, Sadie noted the seat previously occupied by the man was now empty. Turning her attention to finding Josie, she beckoned for Myrtle to follow and headed to the stage door, which she conveniently found open.

One of the stagehands who had been setting tape markings before the rehearsal stopped them once they stepped inside the backstage entrance.

"Are you lost, ladies?" His question was delivered with both curiosity and humor. He hugged his clipboard against his chest and waited for an answer.

"Not lost at all," Sadie said, choosing to take the approach that they not only knew where they were going but were even supposed to be there. "We're meeting Josie. She invited us backstage."

Myrtle nudged her with an elbow, which Sadie ignored. *Just a little white lie.*

"Well, that's easy." He turned and pointed up a small set of stairs. "Just go on up and keep to your left. Her dressing room is down the hallway."

Thanking the stagehand, Sadie and Myrtle followed his directions and soon found the dressing room. Josie and a few other dancers stood around, some with bottles of water. One checked something on her phone. Another arranged makeup and brushes on a dressing table.

Josie smiled as she saw them enter. "You made it! What did you think of the show?"

"It's going to be great," Sadie said. "I can't wait to see you all in full costume." She glanced appreciatively at a rack of sequined outfits nearby, thinking perhaps Coco could use a similar outfit for next Halloween. A flapper Yorkie could be rather novel in a canine costume contest.

"I hope all the stopping and starting didn't bother you too much," Josie said. "Asher's determined to let us know he's the boss now."

"That's for sure," a second dancer said. "Dealing with Seth wasn't exactly a picnic, but he was easier to work with than Asher.

At least he kept things professional during rehearsals, though he was quite the ladies' man outside of work."

Sadie wasn't about to miss an opportunity to fish for more information. "I was wondering about that," she commented casually.

"I fell for it," the second dancer said, rolling her eyes. "I dated him for a month or so."

"So did I," a third dancer called over from a different dressing table.

Sadie looked around, noticing several others raising their hands. She turned her attention back to Josie, who remained quiet.

"At least Seth was entertaining," the second dancer said. "Now we're stuck with Asher."

"Just ignore him," Josie said to the others. "He's just thinks he's *all that* now that he's director."

"Thanks for inviting us to the rehearsal," Sadie said. "It was a treat to be the only ones to see it early."

Myrtle spoke up. "Well, almost the only ones. Aside from that man in the back of the theater."

"Right," Sadie said, looking at Josie. "In the far back corner, on his cell phone."

"That was Bennett," Josie said. "He's a big money guy from the finance office."

"Yep," the second dancer said. "His wife goes to the same nail salon that I go to. She always complains that he works long hours and isn't home enough. Angela is her name, I think."

"Slender, dark red hair?" Myrtle asked.

"Yes."

Myrtle turned to Sadie. "That's the woman he was with in the elevator when he gave me the tickets."

Josie eyed Sadie for permission and then reached into her tote bag to pat Coco on the head. "Well, I'm glad he did so you can see the show. And those VIP packets have a lot of bonuses in them. Or so I hear."

"You're right about that." Myrtle beamed. "Spa treatments, drinks at the Blind Pig, and other discounts."

"Chocolate," Sadie added, not to have the best left out.

"Which reminds me…" Myrtle glanced at a clock on the dressing room wall and turned toward Sadie. "We have appointments at the spa in an hour."

"Sounds wonderful." Josie sighed. "I should get down to the spa soon. My muscles could use it. Not to mention the stress release. We'll need something to detox from working with Asher."

Both of the other dancers nodded in agreement.

"We'll let you get out of here," Sadie said, figuring the showgirls must be eager to go now that the rehearsal was over. "Thanks again for the invite, Josie."

Sadie and Myrtle bid goodbye to the other dancers as well and headed for the exit. Passing the bulletin board they'd seen on their first visit backstage, Sadie slowed down. "Oh, that's disappointing. The shoe sale is over."

Myrtle stopped altogether. "But look at everything in its place."

Sadie took note of the board, which was now covered with detailed directions and changes for the show. "There must be thirty notices here!"

"All signed by Asher," Myrtle noted. "With a flourish! Like an autograph. He certainly got all that organized quickly."

"You're right," Sadie agreed. "*Very* quickly. As if he had all the changes planned already."

Sixteen

Sadie stepped inside the spa and looked around. The cozy space and low ceiling stood in contrast to the expansive nature of the hotel itself. But instead of feeling claustrophobic, it felt comforting, not unlike being wrapped in a soft blanket. Peaceful, soothing music beckoned her forward to a welcome counter with white orchids at one end and a bowl of lavender sachets at the other. The hectic energy and noise of the hotel fell away. She'd stepped into another world.

"May I help you?" A young woman emerged from a hallway, carrying a stack of fluffy cotton robes. She set them on a side table and stepped behind the counter. Her name tag identified her as Becky.

"Yes," Sadie said. "My friend and I have appointments for massages."

Becky ran her finger down a page in the spa's reservation book and stopped at a line corresponding with the current time. "Yes, Sadie and Myrtle. We're ready for you." She peered over Sadie's shoulder, looking for a second person. Sadie adjusted her tote bag on her shoulder, hoping a yip would not emerge.

As if on cue, Myrtle arrived and joined Sadie at the counter.

"See what I told you? Isn't it wonderful in here?" She turned to Becky. "Hello again. I told you I'd bring my friend in."

"Yes, you did," Becky said. "And we're glad to see you both. Your therapists today will be Tawny and Olivia." She glanced at the registration book again. "I see we have you in the double room."

Myrtle nodded. "We wanted that. All the better to visit while being pampered." She and Sadie exchanged grins.

"Well, let's get you set!" Becky gathered two fluffy robes and matching slippers and led them down a hallway, indicating the spa's "quiet room" on the way to a women's locker room. She pointed out lockers and a restroom area and told them to settle in the quiet room once they were ready. The therapists would greet them there. Leaving Sadie and Myrtle to change, she headed back to the reception area.

"I'm glad you suggested this," Sadie said. "What a difference in atmosphere from the hotel." She turned away from Myrtle, partially to allow Myrtle privacy while she changed and partially to perform near physical contortions while trying to put her robe on at the same time as she removed her clothes. She'd always been a bit on the modest side. Except around Coco, of course, who was polite enough to refrain from commenting on what she preferred to think of as her sweet love handles. After a comical amount of squirming, she closed her locker, picked her tote bag back up, and headed for the quiet room. Myrtle soon joined her.

"This is lovely!" Sadie exclaimed as she took in the muted lighting, plush seating area, and carved burl table offering a selection of tea, a glass water dispenser with lemon, lime, and orange slices, and pottery bowls of nuts, crackers, and—she could hardly believe her eyes—chocolate truffles. She helped herself to a glass of chilled water and popped a truffle in her mouth before taking a seat. Closing her eyes, she rested her head against the back cushion and relaxed to the gentle sound of Enya's music.

Several minutes passed before a soft voice spoke. "Ladies, we're ready for you." Sadie looked up to find two women in the doorway, one short with shoulder-length brown hair and a touch more makeup than necessary, the other of medium height with short blond hair and a muscular build that seemed to have "deep tissue" written all over it. Sadie and Myrtle stood and said hello.

"I'm Tawny," the shorter woman said by way of introduction. "Olivia and I will be your therapists today." She gestured to the second woman, who nodded and smiled. "Shall we get started?"

Sadie stood up and picked up her tote bag. "I'm ready." Myrtle also stood.

Tawny eyed Sadie's tote. "Oh, you can leave that in the locker room. We can give you a second locker if it didn't fit in the one with your clothes."

"That's okay." Sadie hugged the tote close. "She, I mean I, prefer to keep it with me."

"Not a problem," Tawny said. "There's a hook in the therapy room. You can hang it up or leave it in the counter."

"Perfect," Sadie said. She and Myrtle followed the two women down a hallway. Myrtle glanced at Sadie's tote bag and rolled her eyes, causing Sadie to fight back a laugh.

After passing through a hallway decorated with soothing floral artwork that reminded Sadie of Georgia O'Keeffe paintings, they stepped into a luxurious room with low lighting, soft music, and two massage tables draped with crisp, white sheets. A hint of lavender filled the air.

While Tawny and Olivia stepped out of the room to allow them privacy to change, Sadie and Myrtle slipped out of their robes and slid under the sheets, relaxing face down. The therapists returned after a polite knock on the door to confirm Sadie and Myrtle were ready. After choosing light oil for their massages—Sadie picked eucalyptus while Myrtle chose an orange blossom scent—the treatments began.

Sadie felt Tawny's hands apply pressure below her neck and slide over her shoulders. As the motion continued along her back, she could feel her tension release. She inhaled deeply, exhaled slowly, and let herself relax into the luxury of the Tawny's expert hands. She rarely treated herself to spa services, not that she couldn't if she wished. San Francisco had excellent day spas with top-notch therapists. It was just one of those things that fell into the "sometime I should" category in life. She had her boutique to run, and there were various social activities that came up, and above all, she generally preferred to spend time at home with Coco.

"Mmm." Myrtle sighed as she enjoyed a similar feeling from the other table. Apparently Olivia had as much of a magic touch as Tawny did.

"Delightful, isn't it?" Sadie said, keeping her voice soft in keeping with the ambiance of the room.

"Perfection," Myrtle agreed. "I told you we needed this."

"You were so right." Sadie took a deep breath again and let it out. "We deserved this."

"Everyone deserves a little spoiling," Tawny said. "Vegas is about more than gambling and shows."

"It certainly is," Sadie agreed. "It seems to be about murder this time."

"You probably brought murder here, Sadie," Myrtle said. "Dead bodies seem to follow you wherever you go."

Sadie felt Tawny's hands hesitate. "Only on a few occasions," Sadie pointed out quickly. "And that's purely a bizarre coincidence, I assure you." She was pleased to feel Tawny resume the massage with renewed confidence.

"Well, you certainly didn't cause the one here," Tawny said.

Sadie's ears perked up. "You're right, of course. I didn't. But what makes you say that?"

"This place is a regular soap opera." Tawny huffed, which resulted in a burst of extra pressure on Sadie's lower back. Admittedly, it felt good, but Sadie was more interested in the conversation. "Someone's always upset about something. Just the other day one of the banquet servers told me the head chef is hot and heavy with the woman who delivers the produce. He'd been seeing the sous chef and then dropped her like a hot potato. The sous chef was so upset she hid the oregano in the walk-in."

"Juicy," Myrtle mumbled. Sadie shushed her and stifled a laugh herself.

"Anyway, that director, Seth, had it coming for a long time," Tawny said as she pressed the heel of one hand into Sadie's calf. "I know I shouldn't speak ill of the dead, but he wasn't the nicest person."

"To whom?" Myrtle mumbled.

Tawny laughed. "A better question would be who *wasn't* angry with him. We hear a lot in here, as you can imagine."

And maybe repeat a lot? Sadie thought. *Maybe a few massages might be in order.*

"Most of the showgirls come in for treatments," Tawny continued. "So do other hotel employees. They get a spa discount. It's one of the perks of working here. We all get discounts in different departments."

Sadie listened closely, pleased for the unexpected opportunity to gather inside information.

"You must hear just about everything that goes on at the Speakeasy," Myrtle said, her words staccato as Olivia leveled chopping motions against her back.

"Not as much as Mason hears," Tawny said. "But I hear a lot."

"Mason?" Sadie hadn't heard this name before now.

"The night bartender at the Blind Pig, also my husband," Tawny offered.

How convenient, Sadie thought. *Another source of clues.*

"You can always count on a bartender for inside information," Tawny continued. "If you can pry the info out, that is."

"How does *he* find out?" Sadie mumbled, relaxing from the massage.

"People tend to talk a lot after having too many drinks. He hears all kinds of things, and then he tells me when he gets home. That's how I found out Seth's room looked like there'd been a fight."

"A fight?" Sadie asked. That did sound in line with what they'd heard backstage.

"I guess so," Tawny said. "Supposedly the room was a mess. Wouldn't surprise me. Just about everyone who's been in here was mad at Seth for one thing or another."

Tawny prompted both women to turn over and settle on their backs. Olivia removed a tray of chilled cucumber slices from a small refrigerator, and Sadie and Myrtle soon felt the cool, soothing compresses on their eyelids.

Sadie sighed as Tawny worked gentle pressure along her upper arms. The combination of cucumber, gentle massage, and soft music was almost enough to put her to sleep. And she might very well have drifted off if she hadn't become aware of a slight percussive element that began to intertwine with the music, a crunching sound. It was almost as if...

"Oh!" Tawny squealed, confirming Sadie's worst suspicions. Sadie turned her head to the side, and the cucumber slices slid off her eyelids. As she feared, the source of the percussive sounds was contentedly sitting next to the tray of cucumber, chomping away.

"Coco!" Sadie sat up, apologizing and wrapping the sheet around her at the same time.

"Now I get it," Tawny said, shaking her head. "This is why you didn't want to leave your bag in a locker. But we can't have pets in the treatment room. I'm sure you understand. Health regulations and all that."

"Of course," Sadie said. "I'll just grab my robe and tote."

"And dog," Tawny prompted. "Don't forget the dog."

"Yes, and the dog." Encouraging Myrtle to finish her treatment, Sadie apologized to Tawny and tiptoed out, one cucumber-munching Yorkie in her arms. She dressed quickly in the locker room, left a generous gratuity for Tawny at the desk, and headed out.

SEVENTEEN

"So now you've been kicked out of the casino *and* the spa. Will we be adding this place to your list?" Myrtle chided Sadie as they took seats at the rich mahogany counter in the Blind Pig. Myrtle slipped onto the barstool to Sadie's right, while Sadie set her tote bag on the seat to her left. Spurred on by Tawny's comment that the bartender was often in the know about what went on in the hotel, they'd donned their spiffiest outfits, entered the bar with the whispered "giggle water" password, and now hoped to do a little information gathering.

"I hope not." Sadie reached into her tote and patted Coco on the head. "Not that I was kicked out of either place, really."

"Whatever you say." Myrtle grinned and then summoned the bartender over when he finished serving a customer at the other end of the bar. To both Sadie and Myrtle's delight, the man who approached had a name tag that said MASON. Just who they were hoping to find.

"What can I get you ladies?" Mason, an attractive, dark-haired man wearing suspenders and a bow tie—Sadie pegged him as being in his midthirties—placed two cocktail napkins on the counter, one in front of each one of them. Sadie looked approvingly at the design on them, a vintage sketch of an automobile appropriate to the 1920s theme.

"A Duesenberg Model J," Sadie said.

"That's not a drink." Myrtle looked at Sadie before turning back to the bartender. "Is it?"

Sadie tapped her index finger on the napkin. "*This*, Myrtle. *This* is a Duesenberg Model J."

"You know your cars," Mason said, impressed. "Not many customers recognize that exact model."

"My third husband was fond of vintage cars," Sadie explained.

"Not her first or second..." Myrtle quipped. Sadie nudged her with an elbow, and Mason fought back a grin.

"We often went to car shows. Car museums, too, when we could."

"Good memories, I bet," Mason said, waiting patiently for them to order.

Sadie perused a table tent menu of cocktails associated with the roaring twenties, reading a few of the selections to Myrtle. "How about a Mary Pickford?" Sadie suggested.

"Hmm." Myrtle looked over the ingredients. "Rum, pineapple juice, grenadine, and maraschino syrup? Sounds a little sweet to me."

"Not for me," Sadie announced, nodding her approval to Mason. "That'll hold my sweet tooth over until I get ahold of some more chocolate."

"What do you suggest, Mason?" Myrtle looked to the bartender for advice. "Something very 1920s to fit the theme around us."

"Maybe a Sidecar or Gin Rickey. Or how about a Bee's Knees?" Mason suggested. "Gin with a bit of honey and lemon juice. A little more on the sour side than your friend's drink will be."

Sadie sighed as Myrtle's face lit up. "Go ahead and say it, Myrtle."

"That sounds like the bee's knees!" Myrtle beamed. "The Bee's Knees is the bee's knees!"

"I bet you've never heard that before." Sadie grinned at Mason.

"Maybe once or twice." Mason winked and turned away to prepare their drinks.

Sadie looked around, impressed once again with the ambiance of the bar. The low lights and dark decor made it easy to imagine they were back in time, snug in a Prohibition-era speakeasy. An old recording of "Sweet Georgia Brown" was just finishing up on the sound system. As "If You Knew Susie" started up right after that, Sadie watched a familiar man enter the bar. Recognizing him immediately from the casino, Sadie turned back to the counter and hoped he didn't veer in their direction but to no avail. He took a seat to her left, separated from them by only the seat her tote bag occupied.

"What'll it be, Dylan?" Mason asked as he delivered Sadie and Myrtle's drinks. "Are you still on the clock?"

"Nope. My shift just ended." Dylan threw some money on the counter. "Beer. Not draft. Give me a bottle of whatever's cheapest."

Mason fetched the bottle and delivered it, lowering his voice as he lifted the money off the counter. "Bennett was looking for you last night. Just thought you'd want to know."

Sadie's ears perked up. Perhaps they'd get some information out of this bar visit after all if the two men continued talking. However, Mason walked away, and Dylan stood, taking his beer from the counter. He glanced at Sadie as he tucked the beer inside his jacket, clearly planning to leave.

"Aren't you the lady I threw out of the casino the other day?" Dylan glanced suspiciously at Sadie's tote bag.

"I was *escorted* out," Sadie huffed, pulling her tote bag closer. "It's not the same thing."

"Whatever you say." He turned and left, passing Josie, who was on her way in.

Josie approached the bar, ordered a beer, and then waved Sadie and Myrtle over to a table that was more private than the bar counter.

"I saw you talking to Dylan," Josie said as Sadie and Myrtle settled in at a table with her. She leaned forward and lowered her voice as she spoke. "You don't want anything to do with him. He's a real snake of a human being, not anyone you want to mess with. He's almost as much of a snake as Seth was."

Details, Sadie thought. She exchanged a glance with Myrtle and was sure they were thinking the same thing. *Details! We need details!*

As if hearing the unspoken request, Josie looked around, noted that no one else was near their table, and then continued. "Seth was seeing Stacey for a while but then started seeing Brandi, though neither one knew he was seeing the other."

A sleazy move on Seth's part, Sadie thought, seeing them both at the same time. *Did they want to get back at him? Vengeance could take many forms. Like murder, for instance.*

"And then Dylan got involved with Brandi?"

Josie nodded. "Yep. Right away. I think he'd been trying to steal Brandi away from Seth for a while. And Seth was none too happy about it."

"So there was conflict between Seth and Dylan then," Sadie said.

"Whew!" Myrtle exclaimed. "Sounds complicated."

Josie laughed. "It's nothing compared to other things that go on here. There's more drama in this place than you can imagine. It's certainly not limited to the theater. Anyway, they both figured it out and decided they'd had enough of Seth's two-timing. So they both dumped him."

"At the same time?" Sadie said. *Impressive.*

Josie nodded. "Seemed awfully coincidental to not be a coordinated effort." She took a draw from the beer bottle and set it back on the table. "I think the two of them were in on it together. Dumping him, that is. Served him right."

Myrtle's eyebrows lifted. "That would explain why..." She turned to Sadie.

"...why they seemed to be getting along perfectly well the other day." Sadie finished Myrtle's sentence for her.

"The other day?" Josie looked back and forth between Sadie and Myrtle.

"Zip-lining," Myrtle said. "We foll... er, happened to see them heading that direction while we were shopping. So we decided to go. It seemed like something fun to try."

Sadie coughed.

"Ooh, you're braver than I am!" Josie exclaimed. She shook her head, dangling earrings flying along with the motion. "I don't do heights. Those crazy zip-lines scare the heck out of me! I turned a job down once that required an aerial number with a harness. Would have been good money too, but no way."

"It wasn't as scary as I thought it would be," Myrtle said. "I'd probably do it again."

"Speak for yourself!" Sadie shook her head from side to side. "Never again for me. Or Coco for that matter."

Josie eyed the tote bag. "I don't even want to know."

"Say." Myrtle leaned in toward Josie. "The bartender just told that guy who left..."

"Dylan," Sadie said.

"Right. He said Bennett was looking for him last night."

Josie nodded. "We don't have much interaction with Bennett. The show cast, I mean."

"Sounds like Dylan might," Sadie suggested, hoping Josie might spill more information.

Josie shrugged. "I guess so. I mean, as floor manager he deals with money."

"And I bet the casino rolls through a ton of it," Myrtle said.

"You'd better believe it." Josie stood, finished most of her beer, and set the bottle on the table. "Anyway, that's the scoop. Enjoy the rest of your evening."

"Well!" Sadie said once she and Myrtle were alone. "That was interesting. I wonder if Dylan and Bennett are connected beyond the daily accounting of casino income."

"Could be. I wouldn't be surprised."

"I'm sure a lot goes on behind the scenes here," Sadie said.

Myrtle stirred her Bee's Knees cocktail and nodded. "And maybe the two of them had some kind of connection to the show —and its director."

Sadie drummed her fingertips against the tabletop. "Did you feel like Josie started backing off the conversation once talk of Bennett came up?"

Myrtle took a sip of her drink and nodded, which proved to be an awkward combination of movements. "Maybe. Maybe not."

Sadie raised her Mary Pickford cocktail in the air, and the two clicked their drinks together.

"I guess we'll just have to find out if Dylan and Bennett are up to something," Myrtle said. "And if Seth had something to do with it."

"Yes," Sadie agreed. "I guess we will."

EIGHTEEN

Sadie approached the hotel's front desk, pleased to have caught it at a time no one was in line. She stepped up to the counter, recognizing the woman working as Cassie, the one who had checked her in originally.

"Sadie Kramer, room 428."

"Yes, Ms. Kramer. What can I do for you today?"

"We're due to check out tomorrow, but we just found out the show opening has been rescheduled. Would it be possible for us to extend our stay?" Sadie waited as Cassie turned to her computer screen and tapped away at the keys, scanning the screen between bursts of taps.

"Not a problem, Ms. Kramer. I'll be happy to extend it."

"And the room next door?" Sadie added quickly. "My friend is staying there. It's also in my name."

After more clicking of the keyboard, Cassie confirmed she had extended both rooms.

"Excellent," Sadie exclaimed. "We're thrilled we'll get to see the show. It was terrible that it was canceled. Of course, I mean terrible the reason it was canceled."

"Yes," Cassie said. "We're all shocked."

"Have the police figured out what happened yet?" It was worth a try asking, Sadie thought. One never knew where information might be found.

Cassie shook her head. "If they have, we haven't been told. Management has just encouraged us to carry on as normal."

"Of course," Sadie said. "That makes sense. Thanks so much for extending the room reservations."

"My pleasure," Cassie said.

Sadie moved away from the desk and stopped by the coffee kiosk. She ordered a latte, took a seat at one of the tables in the kiosk area, and pulled out her phone. She'd been wanting to check in with Amber, her store manager, but now needed to tell her she'd be back two days later than planned. After two rings, Amber picked up.

"Amber, my favorite shop manager!" Sadie exclaimed as Amber answered.

"I'm your only shop manager." Amber laughed.

"All the more reason for you to be my favorite, my dear." Sadie smiled. "How's everything going?"

"A little slow but we've still had quite a few sales. Mrs. Wheatley bought that thick cable cardigan that we've been displaying in the window."

"Good choice for her." Sadie knew her regular customers, and this one was a fan of bulky sweaters.

"Scarf sales have been good too, thanks to those new ones we got in. We're already sold out of turquoise."

Sadie wasn't surprised. She'd known those pashmina scarves would be popular, especially with all the colors they had in stock. She made a mental note to order more in turquoise when she got back as well as extras in other colors.

"It's no surprise to me that everything's going well," Sadie said. "I never worry when you're there. Speaking of which, I've extended my stay here two more days. I hope that works for you. If not, I can cancel."

"That's wonderful," Amber replied. "Of course that works for me. I'm here those days anyway. I take it you and Myrtle are having a great time."

"Indeed, we are. And I'll have some stories to tell when I get back."

"You always do." Sadie could hear Amber trying not to laugh. "Speaking of which, Broussard called to check on you. He said he's forbidden to call you on a girl's weekend."

"Yes, that was the plan." Sadie laughed. "Though I might give him a call. Something came up after we checked in."

"Not again," Amber said.

"I'm afraid so." Sadie knew Amber was familiar with the tendency for dead bodies to show up on Sadie's trips.

"There's never a dull moment when you're out and about."

"It doesn't appear so, does it?"

"Dare I ask who the unfortunate person was this time?"

Sadie sighed. Her reputation for falling into these situations was well established. "It was the show director for the production at this hotel. He was found in his room on what should have been the opening night."

"Not alive, I assume," Amber said.

"No, unfortunately."

"And what is the name of the detective you're harassing this time?" Amber laughed, and Sadie could only accept the well-deserved teasing.

"His name's Tanner," Sadie said. "He actually seems like a nice guy. As detectives go, that is. Walks like Charlie Chaplin."

"That must be amusing."

"It is." Sadie chuckled. "He fits right in with the theme here."

They exchanged a few more pleasantries, and Sadie thanked Amber for watching the store. Ending the phone call, she spotted Myrtle across the lobby and caught up with her in time to ride the elevator to their rooms together. Once on their floor, they started down the hall only to find a familiar figure waiting.

"Detective Tanner," Sadie said as they approached, hoping she sounded as nonchalant as she intended. "How lovely to see you." *Another little white lie. I really shouldn't make a habit of this.*

The detective leaned casually against the wall, not at all coincidentally across from Sadie and Myrtle's rooms.

"Has this become your favorite hallway?" Sadie quipped.

"It has its charms," the detective said. "And it's hopefully a source of information."

Sadie raised her eyebrows and exchanged a look with Myrtle. "In that case, we're all ears, Detective. What information do you have for us?"

The detective cleared his throat, and something close to a frown spread across his face. "So now you're a comedian in addition to being an amateur detective."

"Oh!" Sadie beamed. "Is that what I am? A detective? Do I get a badge?"

Detective Tanner seemed less than impressed with Sadie's humor. "I take that back. I don't think you're a comedian *or* a detective, amateur or otherwise. I think you're someone here on vacation who'd be wise to stick to vacation activities. I hear the casino has ample entertainment to keep you busy."

"She's already been thrown out of there," Myrtle offered, earning a reproachful glance from Sadie.

"I see." Tanner's normally serious expression was replaced with a look of amusement.

"It wasn't quite like that," Sadie said. "It was really my dog who got thrown out."

"The one who has a passion for shoelaces?" Tanner said, his voice remarkably deadpan.

"And then she got thrown out of the spa," Myrtle added.

"Myrtle!" Sadie looked at her friend with surprise. "Whose friend are you?"

"Yours, Sadie, of course," Myrtle assured her. "I'm just stating facts."

Detective Tanner seemed to perk up at this. "Facts are my

business. Perhaps before I ask you *again* to stay out of this matter, you might have something of interest to tell me."

"Like what?" Sadie said.

"Like something you might have heard this morning at breakfast. That young lady came over to your table after what appeared to be an uncomfortable conversation."

Sadie tapped her chin dramatically as if trying to remember. Myrtle did the same.

"No reason to play coy, ladies," the detective said. "You know exactly who I mean."

Sadie nodded. "Yes, that's Josie, a showgirl we've gotten to know. She stopped by on her way out. The man she was talking to —and not very fondly—is the new show director, Asher. It seems he jumped at the chance to take over that role."

"He was the assistant director before," Myrtle added. "But he always wanted to be director." She leaned forward and lowered her voice. "That's a motive, right?"

"It could be," Tanner said lightly. "But it also might not be. It's not unusual for people to want to move up into higher positions. For better pay, if nothing else. Or in the case of show business, ego."

"But," Sadie pointed out, "they don't all have huge arguments with the higher-up person the night before he's, well, you know."

Tanner pulled a notebook and pen from his pocket. "And you know this how?"

"Josie told us," Sadie said. "When she explained how badly he wanted the director job."

Myrtle nodded. "Yes, *how* badly is the question." She looked at Sadie. "But you also said Josie and Seth argued a lot for the same reason. She was upset about not getting solo roles."

"You two do seem to have a line to inside information," Tanner said. Sadie noted a touch of jealousy in the detective's words.

"But we're not law enforcement," Sadie pointed out.

"I'm rather pleased to hear that you know that."

"What I *mean* is," Sadie said somewhat emphatically, "that some people are more willing to talk to a casual stranger than to an officer. Authority figures can make people nervous."

Tanner sighed. "Well, we shouldn't. We're just doing our job, trying to help."

"I know that, and you know that," Sadie said. "I'm just saying how it is. For example, as a kid, did you ever get called into the principal's office? Perhaps even when you hadn't done anything wrong?"

Tanner tilted his head to the side, thinking back. "Yes, I do remember a time or two like that. I was a bit of a troublemaker growing up."

Sadie sensed a certain amount of pride in his statement, and she fought back a grin. "And how did you feel?"

"Uncomfortable."

"Even when you'd done nothing wrong?"

Tanner nodded. "Now that you mention it, yes. I just wanted to get out of there."

"Right," Sadie said. "Not because you'd done anything wrong but simply because it was an authority figure, therefore somewhat intimidating."

"I see your point."

"This means we can be useful to you!" Myrtle piped up enthusiastically. "We can be junior detectives!"

Tanner shook his head adamantly. "Absolutely not. However... I may stop by periodically for a casual chat. You do seem to come up with some potentially helpful bits of information." He put his notepad and pen back in his pocket.

Myrtle leaned toward Sadie and quietly whispered, "Like I said, junior detectives." Tanner frowned but pretended not to have heard.

"Good night, ladies." The detective ambled down the hallway toward the elevator.

"Oh, and Detective?" Sadie called after Tanner, who turned around, his expression half guarded and half curious. "If you're looking for inside information, you might think about getting a massage in the spa here. Ask for Tawny."

Delighted with the look of sheer confusion on the detective's face, Sadie waved, and she and Myrtle slipped back into their rooms.

Nineteen

Sadie rummaged through her closet, searching for an outfit she hadn't yet worn on this trip. Although adding two extra days to their stay was a perfect excuse to go shopping, it wasn't going to happen before breakfast. And breakfast was certainly going to come before a shopping excursion.

Opting for a rather boring—in her opinion—red tunic and a flouncy black skirt, she dressed this up with oversized parrot earrings that dangled close to her shoulders. She fluffed her hair and stood back from the closet mirror, inspecting the overall look.

"I approve," Myrtle said as she stepped into the room by way of the adjoining door. She had chosen a similar style of dress for the morning, although her skirt was a floral print and her tunic a turquoise hue that picked up one of the bright colors in her skirt. In contrast to Sadie's whimsical parrot earrings, Myrtle had donned simple clip-on purple enamel squares with a slightly bumpy texture.

"Don't we look the pair?" Sadie exclaimed. A yip from Coco, who stood back as if inspecting them both, offered agreement.

"Let's get you spruced up too, Coco," Sadie said, picking up a brush reserved for the petite Yorkie. After giving Coco's fur a once-over, she opened a zip bag, rummaged through in search of an accessory, and came up with a glittery pink polka-dot bow. She clipped the bow to the top of Coco's head, and the three headed out. They were soon seated in Gatsby's Grill, just as they had been the morning before and likely would be the following morning.

"You can't beat the selection here," Myrtle said as she took a seat and eyed the buffet.

Sadie nodded as she settled into a seat across from Myrtle. She set her tote bag, precious cargo included, on the chair beside her. She made what she hoped was a casual reconnaissance perusal of the breakfast crowd.

"Expecting anyone?" Myrtle asked. She unrolled a napkin from the silverware setup on her side of the table. "Hoping to see someone? Hoping *not* to see someone?"

"Hmm." Sadie brought her gaze back to Myrtle. "Now that you put it that way, I suppose I might hope to see Josie or even Brandi. And hopefully *not* Detective Tanner. He's more of a hindrance than a help."

Myrtle smiled. "I'm quite sure that feeling is mutual, though he was rather cordial last night in the hallway."

"True," Sadie admitted. "I've certainly had worse encounters with detectives."

"And much *nicer* ones." Myrtle grinned, referring to Sadie's favorite New Orleans member of law enforcement.

Sadie brushed the comment away even as she felt a blush creeping up her neck. It had been ages since she'd seen Detective Broussard, and she missed him. A trip to the Big Easy in the near future might not be a bad idea.

Tote bag in tow, the women headed to the buffet and soon returned to the table with their chosen breakfast fare. Sadie had been delighted to find a jalapeño egg casserole, bacon, and home fries while Myrtle chose silver dollar pancakes—she loved the miniature size—with sliced strawberries. Both helped themselves to juice, and the same server they'd had the day before left water and coffee for both of them while they were at the buffet.

"What did you think about Josie's comments in the bar

yesterday?" Sadie asked as she stuck a fork into her casserole. "About Brandi and Stacey?" She tore off a piece of bacon and held her hand inside her tote, soon feeling an expected chomp near her fingertips.

"I'm not sure what to think," Myrtle said. "It sounds complicated. We know they get along. We've seen them together outside of work. I guess the musical relationships with the guys hasn't hurt their friendship."

"It doesn't seem like it," Sadie said. "Otherwise, they wouldn't get together outside of work. I wonder how Dylan fits into the picture."

"Honestly, that guy gives me the creeps." Myrtle lowered her voice. "Not only because he threw... I mean, had you escorted out of the casino. But he acted cagey in the bar."

"Maybe." Sadie thought this over. "He seemed a little bent out of shape. Do you think he had something to do with Seth's murder?"

Myrtle shrugged. "Who knows? He's now seeing Seth's ex. Maybe there was a little jealousy going on between them."

"It's possible."

"Maybe the casino and theater are connected," Myrtle said. "They're under the same roof, but are they connected financially?"

Sadie's eyebrows lifted. "Good question. Maybe everything in the hotel is managed by the same finance people. That would mean..."

"...that Dylan and Bennett could be up to no good," Myrtle finished.

"The bartender did tell Dylan that Bennett was looking for him," Sadie said. "That seemed a little odd."

"Not necessarily. I mean, Dylan is the floor manager, so he must have something to do with the money." Myrtle headed to the buffet for more sliced strawberries, returning with extras for Sadie.

"I'm not sure how much," Sadie said as Myrtle settled back in.

"The cashier would be the one who actually handles the cash. And not everything is purchased with cash."

"True. I hardly ever use cash anymore. Credit cards are much easier. But the cashier would have a record of what comes in and goes out, probably very carefully monitored."

Sadie nodded. "I'm sure that's true. Which brings me to wonder who monitors that. Would it be the floor manager? Or another supervisor? Someone would have to."

Myrtle tapped the end of her fingers on the table. "So who would that be?"

Sadie stabbed a strawberry with her fork. "We need to find out."

TWENTY

The Blind Pig was hopping when Sadie and Myrtle slid in during the late afternoon. Happy hour specials had started, always a way to drum up business in a watering hole. Upbeat jazz music flowed from the overhead speakers, and an enthusiastic party atmosphere floated around the room.

Sadie and Myrtle took a seat at a table not far from the bar, avoiding the counter seats in order to converse without being overheard. A cocktail server was on duty—a sweet young lady in her twenties wearing a sparkling silver beaded drop-waist dress with a stylish feathered headband around her forehead—so they ordered the Bee's Knees and Mary Pickford drinks that they'd had before, delighted to find them half price at that hour.

"Appetizers?" Myrtle looked over the table tent menu. "Moonshine Mozzarella Sticks, Prohibition Potato Skins, Speakeasy Sliders, Fly Boy Cheese Fries."

"I'm still full from breakfast," Sadie said. "I can wait until dinner."

"Same." Myrtle set the menu down and thanked the server, who headed off to fetch their cocktails.

A rendition of "Bye Bye Blackbird" came over the sound

system, followed by "Ain't Misbehavin'" as Sadie and Myrtle took advantage of people-watching. Establishments such as the one they were in were perfect for that.

Their flapper-styled server returned with their drinks, which Sadie charged to her hotel room. "My treat today," Sadie said to Myrtle as she tipped the server in cash. They clinked their glasses together and took initial sips.

"Hey, there's Coco's favorite casino dealer." Myrtle nodded toward the door as Brandi entered. Coco yipped at the sound of her own name. Brandi waved at Sadie and Myrtle and then headed for the bar. Mason, clearly expecting her request, grabbed a cup from a stack of plastic drink ware and filled it with soda. Brandi pulled money out of her pocket, but he waved it away. With a casual "Thanks, Mason," she strolled over to Sadie and Myrtle's table. Sadie gestured for her to sit, taking Coco out of her tote bag and setting her on her lap as added incentive. Just as she hoped, Brandi sat down.

"Working today?" Sadie said. She eyed Brandi's drink, suddenly craving a soda. She'd given up most soda years ago, but she'd never completely kicked the habit. Every now and then the craving kicked in.

"Just on a break," Brandi said as she gave Coco a pat on the head. "Which is a good thing. I needed to get out of there for a bit. Too much drama."

Sadie's ears perked up. Drama was rarely something she wanted to miss, usually just as a matter of curiosity. She'd always had an appreciation for a bit of mayhem. But in this case, it could mean more. Perhaps she could pick up a few clues about Seth's demise.

"What kind of drama?" She watched as Brandi took a sip of soda, envious.

"Rumors," Brandi said, leaning closer. "I never know if anything's true or not. But there's always something."

Sadie leaned forward as well. "Like what in particular?"

Brandi shrugged. "I don't know. About a week ago I overheard one of the cashiers talking in the restroom. Something to do with shady money dealings, but she wasn't sure. I tried to find out more from Dylan, and he told me to mind my own business. Not in so many words, but he brushed it off. I could tell he didn't want to talk about it."

Myrtle and Sadie exchanged glances, clearly thinking the same thing. *Could this have something to do with Seth's murder?*

"The floor manager, the guy with no sense of humor," Sadie noted. "The guy who has people escorted from the casino for no reason." She was more than familiar with Dylan after Coco's casino escapade.

"Yeah, he can be a bit much," Brandi said. "But he's not always like that. Outside of work, he's usually fine. It's just in the casino that he's on edge." She pushed her chair back and stood up. "Speaking of which, I'd better get back. Break's almost over. You should come into the casino today. Maybe let that cute pup take another spin."

"And tangle with Dylan again?" Sadie laughed. "No thanks."

"Oh, he's not working today," Brandi said. "Someone else is filling in. He had a bit of a... situation last night. I'll leave it at that. In any case, you're safe in the casino today." She leaned close to Sadie's tote bag and added, "And so are you." She glanced at the clock, said a quick goodbye, and hurried out.

"Well, that was interesting," Sadie said, turning to Myrtle. "What kind of situation do you think she meant?"

Myrtle shrugged. "Something that would keep him from work today, I guess. Maybe a night of overindulgence? He could be nursing a hangover today."

"Or something more serious that Brandi didn't feel like talking about." Sadie took a sip of her drink. "It's like it slipped out and then she realized she didn't want to explain."

"I think she was just in a rush to get back to work," Myrtle said. "But if you stop into the casino like she said, you might be able to find out more."

"Worth a try," Sadie agreed. "If nothing else, I can check out whatever drama she's talking about."

Myrtle nodded. "I think most workplaces have some sort of drama going on even if just to make the job more interesting. I worked in an office once where there were new rumors being spread around almost every day. Most were little things like accusations about lunches disappearing from the fridge. But some were serious. Inappropriate relationships between employees and management, that kind of thing. I doubt even half of them were remotely true."

"You have a point." Sadie could think of a few times she'd seen this happen. "But if there is something fishy going on with money, that could be important right now. Money's often a motive in crime, and it could definitely be in the case of murder."

Myrtle tapped her fingers against her glass while pondering the possibilities. "Do you think something was going on between Dylan, Bennett, and Seth? Were all three of them in on something together?"

"I guess it's a possibility," Sadie said. "It would have to be something that involved all their positions. Maybe money connections between the casino and theater?"

"Could be. Or it might have nothing to do with money. Maybe this is just between Dylan and Seth," Myrtle pointed out. "Brandi's ex and her current flame. That could be a recipe for jealousy."

"That's also not unusual as a motive for crime," Sadie said. "But Brandi and Seth weren't seeing each other anymore. If anything, Seth would have been jealous of Dylan because she's now seeing him. So I don't see a jealousy motive for Dylan."

"What about the money motive?" Myrtle asked.

"It's possible, I guess. But only if someone had something to gain by Seth's death." Sadie frowned. "We need more information." Sadie finished her drink and set the glass down on the table.

"And I have a feeling you're on your way to get it."

Sadie stood, grabbed her tote bag, and pushed in her chair. "You know it. I'd like to find out exactly what 'situation' Dylan got into." Arranging to meet up with Myrtle later, she headed out, the casino as her destination.

Twenty-One

Sadie stepped into the casino, pausing to let her eyes adjust to the sharp contrast in light from the lobby. While the hotel's lobby was bright and welcoming, the casino's subdued atmosphere boasted soft, low light, burgundy carpeting, and dark wood gaming tables. It felt like entering another world, which wasn't far from the truth. In fact, it felt like forbidden territory after her first visit, which just added to the ambiance. She loved it.

"Here we are, Coco," she whispered to her tote bag. "You need to behave this time. Do we have a deal?" A yip followed, though Sadie wasn't sure if it was in agreement or rebuttal. At least Dylan wouldn't be there to have them escorted out.

With Myrtle back at the spa for another treatment, Sadie was on her own. She looked around, spotted Brandi, and wandered over to the roulette table where Brandi was biding her time between customers. Sadie set her tote bag on the edge of the table, knowing Brandi would want to pet Coco, who stuck her head out, eyed the roulette wheel suspiciously, and retreated quickly. As expected, Brandi reached into the tote and gave Coco a scrunch behind the ears. She and Sadie both laughed, realizing how odd that would look to anyone passing by.

"No customers?" Sadie said, noting the empty table.

"Not at the moment." Brandi leaned one hip against the table. "It'll get busy again. Activity comes and goes in here. It's rarely consistent."

Sadie picked up on Brandi's lack of enthusiasm and couldn't help asking an obvious question.

"If you weren't working here, what would you be doing?"

Brandi shifted her weight from one foot to the other, pondering the question. "Probably something in the medical field. Some kind of technician maybe. I'd like to work in a hospital setting. I've looked into training programs. I've been saving money to enroll."

"That sounds wonderful," Sadie said. "I have a lot of respect for healthcare workers. Not an easy job. But rewarding. I hope it works out for you."

"Thanks."

"You mentioned Dylan got into some kind of situation last night," Sadie said, phrasing it as a statement in hopes she didn't sound too pushy.

Brandi sighed. "Yeah, it was ridiculous but upsetting."

"Sorry to hear that," Sadie said as nonchalantly as possible. *Go on, go on!*

"I guess I can tell you." Brandi's gaze floated around the room, and Sadie couldn't help but wonder if she was searching for potential customers or something else. "It looked serious at the time, but I don't think it could have been." Brandi looked almost convinced that she believed her own words.

And? Sadie thought, hoping to hear more. Fortunately for Sadie, she continued.

"A couple of policemen showed up wanting to question him."

"Here?" Sadie felt her breath hitch, and she felt guilty for her reaction. On one hand, she knew that had to have been upsetting for Brandi. On the other hand, this was juicier than expected and also potentially instrumental to finding out what happened to Seth.

Brandi nodded. "Yes, here in the casino. It was embarrassing. For him, of course, but also for everyone watching."

"So they questioned him here?"

"No, they took him down to the station. I don't know exactly where. He sent me a text later and said he was home and fine, that it was nothing important."

"Well, that's good then," Sadie said. "Isn't it? If he was in some kind of trouble, they would have kept him."

"I guess so." Brandi turned to the table and brushed a bit of dust off. "But he wouldn't tell me what it was about, which bothered me. He used to tell me everything, but not lately. He just said he wouldn't be at work today. It's out of character for him."

"In what way?" Sadie asked, hoping she wasn't pushing too hard.

"Well, for one thing, he never misses a day of work. Ever. And he's usually very open with me, so it's odd he wouldn't tell me why they took him down to the station. But there was something else that was odd."

"What was that?"

Brandi sighed. "It was a little thing, at least I thought so. Now I'm not so sure. I'd overheard something Dylan said on a phone call a few days earlier."

"About Seth?"

Brandi shook her head. "No, about Bennett. I didn't hear much. I only heard Dylan mention Bennett's name, saying they 'almost had him.' Whatever that was supposed to mean. I figured it might have to do with the production budget. Seth had been worried about that, so I thought he should know what I overheard. So I went to see him."

"I hope you don't mind me asking this," Sadie said. "Was this the night before he was found? When you told him?"

Brandi gasped. "I didn't kill him! You can even ask Stacey. She knows I was only going to warn him about what I heard."

"Oh, I wasn't implying you did!" Sadie said quickly. "I just wondered what kind of mood he was in, what his frame of mind was."

Brandi looked around to see if anyone might be listening. She then turned back to Sadie, lowering her voice. "Yes, I saw him that night. We stayed on friendly terms after we stopped dating. He wasn't really the jerk people thought he was." She brushed a tear away. "He was actually a decent guy. He just got carried away sometimes. He had some anger issues and wasn't patient with people."

"How did he seem that night when you saw him? Did he act like anything was wrong?"

Brandi shook her head. "Not at first. He was in a good mood, looking forward to the show opening."

"And then what changed?"

"I told him what I'd overheard, and he got upset, like, *really* upset."

"Arguments about money are bound to happen in business," Sadie said. "Maybe the show was running over budget, and he was under pressure because of it." Sadie played with this thought for a minute. Bennett could easily have blamed Seth for money problems if he felt he wasn't running the show well.

"I wouldn't be surprised," Brandi said. "Shows often run over budget. It's Vegas, you know. People want bigger and better, flashier and impressive. That costs money."

"But this seemed like more than their usual disagreements?"

Brandi nodded. "I knew he'd been fighting with Bennett over the show budget. They argued a lot about little things like costumes costing too much or tech people being paid more than necessary. But this seemed like something more than their normal spats. He said something about how Bennett was pressuring him and that he was sick and tired of it. He said he was going to go to the authorities. But I wonder..."

Sadie watched Brandi clam up, holding back whatever she was about to say. "What do you wonder?"

"I don't want to think this, I really don't..." Again, Brandi's voice trailed off.

"Maybe it could be helpful, Brandi," Sadie said. "What is it?"

"I wonder if Seth confronted Bennett instead of going directly to the police," Brandi finally said. "Or maybe Dylan went to talk to Seth himself. And maybe that... didn't go well?" Her eyes teared up again.

"You don't think..." Sadie didn't want to say the words.

"No!" Brandi exclaimed. "Dylan would never hurt anyone! He's not that type of person!"

Is anyone really the type before they become the type? Sadie thought.

Sadie reached out at touched her Brandi's arm gently. "I'm sorry. I didn't mean to upset you." She fished a tissue out of her tote bag and offered it.

"It's okay," Brandi said as she took the tissue. "I want to know what happened as much as anyone else."

"I suspect the truth will come out at some point," Sadie said, reassuring her. "It usually does."

Twenty-Two

"Oh, have I got a scoop for you," Sadie announced as she caught up with Myrtle at the coffee kiosk.

"Really? Because I have a scoop for you too," Myrtle countered. "But you go first."

"No, you," Sadie said.

"No, *you*," Myrtle urged. "Okay, I'll go first. Tawny was quite the chatterbox during my spa treatment."

Sadie's eyebrows raised. "Really? Do tell."

"It turns out both Brandi and Stacey were in for spa treatments recently."

"Together?" Sadie asked. "Like when we went in?"

Myrtle shook her head. "No. Individually, which is great because they were more loose-lipped than they would have been in each other's presence."

"And?" Sadie urged Myrtle to continue.

"And apparently things haven't always been as friendly between them." Myrtle leaned forward and lowered her voice as if imparting knowledge of top-secret government information.

Sadie thought this over. "Maybe they blamed each other for the way Seth played them, trying to date them at the same time."

Myrtle shrugged her shoulders. "I don't doubt it. It sounds

like each one held on at first, making it some kind of competition, each waiting for him to dump the other one."

"But in the end, they both got wise and dumped him," Sadie said.

"Exactly. Because he continued to string them both along," Myrtle explained. "Tawny thinks Brandi gave up first, but Stacey continued trying to win him over."

"But she obviously gave up eventually," Sadie pointed out. "There doesn't seem to be any animosity between them now."

"Maybe they bonded over that experience. You know how it goes. If a guy double-times two women, it's usually the guy who loses in the end. Never underestimate the power of two women teaming up." Myrtle took a sip of her iced drink and looked at Sadie.

"Excellent point," Sadie said.

"But there's more." Myrtle looked around. "Tawny had someone in from the kitchen staff who said the shrimp cocktail came back clean. No poison."

Sadie nodded. "Aha, well that makes sense. The kitchen would need to know right away whether they had to throw food out and whether or not it was safe to serve other dishes."

"So, what's your scoop?" Myrtle asked.

"It's a good one. Let me get a coffee." She made a quick trip to the counter and soon returned with an iced dark chocolate mocha. She settled into her seat and took a slow sip of the icy drink while Myrtle attempted to wait patiently.

"So?" Myrtle pressed.

"Oh, right," Sadie said, emerging from the chocolate trance. "Dylan got picked up by the police last night."

"What? Where? When? Why?" Myrtle scrambled for details.

Sadie laughed. "Are you planning to take up a career in journalism?"

"Well, I already know 'who,'" Myrtle pointed out. "So fill in the rest."

"I actually don't know much more." Sadie took another

lengthy sip of the chocolate drink. "Brandi just told me he was picked up last night in the casino and taken down to the local police station."

"Did they keep him? Book him? Charge him?"

Sadie shook her head. "Apparently, the answer is none of the above. Brandi said he sent her a text later that he was home. That's all."

"Huh. Well, it must not be all," Myrtle said. "There has to be more to the story. Do you think they picked him up for something to do with Seth's murder?"

"I don't think so, at least not with anything concrete," Sadie said. "They would have kept him."

"True. It must have just been for questioning."

"What was just for questioning?" A new voice joined the discussion, and Sadie and Myrtle looked up to see Josie.

"We're exchanging scoops," Sadie said. "Dylan was picked up and taken down to the police station last night. Brandi told me when I was in the casino earlier."

"You're allowed in the casino now?" Josie smirked.

"Very funny," Sadie said, her head tilted slightly to the side. "I see news travels quickly. And yes, as a matter of fact, I am. At least I am when Dylan's not around."

"Ah, I see." Josie nodded. "And he's off today because he was rounded up again last night."

"*Again?*" Sadie and Myrtle exchanged glances. "What do you mean *again*?" Sadie said.

"Yep, again," Josie said, replying to both of them. "They question him from time to time. I think it's to make sure everything on the floor stays on the straight and narrow. He is the floor manager after all."

"Ah, then he's not in trouble," Myrtle said. "It's about casino security."

Josie nodded. "That's my guess. They check all the casinos, I imagine. Vegas isn't exactly a crime-free zone. Especially with the amount of money that flows through."

"So questioning him must have been routine." Sadie said.

"But why did they take him in?" Myrtle asked. "Why not just talk to him right here in the hotel?"

"That's not hard to figure out," Josie said. "Nothing's private in here. The walls have ears, as they say. Everybody's into everybody else's business."

"I can see that," Sadie mused.

"It also doesn't hurt to have customers see the cops come through here now and then," Josie added. "People are less likely to try anything they shouldn't."

"Makes sense," Sadie said. "I always try to behave myself when police are around."

Myrtle chuckled. "And believe me, she gets a lot of practice."

Sadie rolled her eyes.

Josie lowered her voice. "As long as we're exchanging scoops, I have a scoop for you. Evan is opening up a little about when he found Seth. He said..." Josie stopped, tried to force the next words out. "He said Seth had a bad head wound."

"That fits with the poison news," Myrtle said.

Josie's teary eyes flew open. "Poison?"

"In the shrimp cocktail," Sadie clarified.

"Oh, I get it." Josie's expression took on a hint of a smile. "His legendary superstition." She glanced across the lobby, waved to a fellow cast member, and excused herself.

"LOOK," MYRTLE SAID, INDICATING A LARGE HALL WITH double doors propped open. A poster announced the Art Deco exhibition they'd seen on the list of hotel activities. "Let's check it out. We have time to kill. Oops!" Myrtle brought her hand to her mouth, realizing the phrase was perhaps too apropos for their visit.

Sadie grinned. "Fortunately, we're in the clear," she said as she followed Myrtle into the room. "There are enough suspects as it is."

A hotel employee greeted them at the door and welcomed them in to a display that was more expansive than they'd expected. A replica of the Empire State Building graced the center of the floor, rising a good twelve feet in height. Myrtle took a place beside it and had Sadie take a picture of her. They switched places for another picture, and then the employee supervising the exhibition took a photo of them together.

"Now we can say we've been to New York," Myrtle quipped.

"Or we could go to the New York casino just down the street," Sadie pointed out. "Then we could say we went to New York twice on this trip." She glanced at the hotel employee, certain she was trying not to roll her eyes.

Myrtle tapped a placard next to the model. "It's an impressive building. Says here it was built in 1931 and was the tallest building in the world for almost forty years. 'Considered an Art Deco landmark with common themes of geometric patterns, elongated lines, and vertical emphasis.'"

"We have a lot of Art Deco architecture in San Francisco too," Sadie said. "The Golden Gate Bridge, for one. I've driven across that many times. I once helped solve a mystery up in the wine country."

"That must have been fun," Myrtle said. "Did it involve free beverages?"

Sadie smiled. "I'll never tell."

They continued on, browsing the displays, noting examples of graphic design, furniture, textiles, glass art, and jewelry from the period.

"Ooh, I wouldn't mind having this for a fancy outing!" Sadie stopped in front of a photograph of an emerald pendant. "Wouldn't you? Look at the geometric detail of the chain, not to mention the emerald setting itself."

Myrtle caught up to her, having paused to admire a Tiffany lamp that caught her eye. She read the caption on the photo and nodded. "'Mackay Emerald Necklace.' It's lovely, though I doubt I could afford it. Not to mention that breaking into the Smithsonian to get it could be problematic."

"Yes, there's that."

Myrtle checked her phone. "Charleston time. We'd better get over to the room." Thanking the hotel employee for their tour of the exhibit, they headed for the lesson.

TWENTY-THREE

Sadie and Myrtle were surprised to find the hall reserved for the Charleston lesson crowded when they arrived. Several dozen people strolled around the room, and others were arriving. Some of the dancers—or dancers-to-be—practiced steps, whether with partners or on their own. A few of the women wore flapper costumes, indicating that participation was preplanned by some, and even those in street clothes wore some type of adornment, whether a headband, a cloche hat, or a string of beads.

"Look," Myrtle said, grabbing Sadie's arm and pulling her toward a table of accessories. "I need something from here. Maybe a few things. Maybe *lots* of things!" She lifted up a gold sequined headband with a bright purple feather attached that stood a good eight inches high. "How about this?" She then held up a silk head wrap with a peacock brooch sparkling from a knotted section of the fabric. She held one on each side of her head, comparing the two in front of a standing mirror. "What do you think?"

"I like both," Sadie said as she rummaged through other offerings on the table. "Though that peacock brooch is gorgeous!" She lifted up a strand of white beads and held them against herself. "These will do nicely. And that headpiece over there." She reached across to grab an exotic combination of white feathers and rhinestones. Placing the beads around her neck, she secured the flashy headpiece and looked in the mirror, approving of her choices. For good measure, she added gold elbow-length gloves and a white feather boa.

"Now you're styling!" Myrtle exclaimed. Taking a cue from Sadie, she added turquoise gloves, having decided to go with the peacock headpiece. Glancing at the options one last time, she also tossed a feather boa around her shoulders, this one turquoise.

"Well, look at us!" Sadie exclaimed as they both stood in front of the mirror. "I think a picture is in order." Myrtle nodded and pulled her cell phone out of her evening bag. The woman in charge of the accessory table was happy to take a photo of the two of them. As they thanked her and turned away, they heard a familiar voice.

"Good afternoon, dancers!"

Sadie and Myrtle both looked up, delighted to see that Josie would be the instructor. They were thrilled to see her in full flapper regalia with fringe, feathers, and sparkles from head to toe. Rhinestone bracelets picked up similar stones in her stunning teal-and-black flapper dress and the headband that graced her forehead. Even her gold dance shoes had jeweled heels.

"Find a place out on the floor and get ready to have some Charleston fun!"

Stepping around others who were deciding where to stand, Sadie and Myrtle moved forward, positioning themselves midway to the front. Following others, they stretched their arms to the sides to make sure they were adequately spaced and then focused their attention on Josie, who was beginning a series of warm-up exercises.

"Right arm over your head, stretch to the left..." Josie demonstrated the movements with such flexibility that Sadie found herself tilting her head to watch her, though her body was less willing to follow.

"And now to the other side..." Left arms all across the room reached to the right over heads as torsos followed.

"Now roll your shoulders back..." Josie began slow circles up and to the back. "And reverse..."

Sadie and Myrtle exchanged triumphant glances as they rolled their shoulders to the front.

"I can do this!" Sadie whispered.

Myrtle nodded. "It's a snap!"

After similar exercises to loosen up rib cages, hips, and legs, Josie announced it was time to dance.

"Follow along with me," Josie offered. "Tap front, step back together, other foot tap back, step together, and repeat. Feel that rhythm, one, two, three, four. Taps on one and three."

"Easy!" Sadie whispered to Myrtle, who nodded, eyebrows raised as if surprised they were starting off so well.

"Moving on, replace that front tap with a kick." Josie demonstrated, again counting out the beats.

"Still not too bad!" Myrtle said just as she gave an overly exuberant front kick and nearly lost her balance.

"We're doing great!" Sadie agreed.

"Now add your arms," Josie instructed. "Swing them side to side, opposite arm to each leg."

Sadie attempted to add the arm swings and found herself flashing back to the game Twister from her younger years. *Right kick front, left arm swings forward, left kick back, right arm swings.*

"Don't overthink it," Josie cautioned. "This is the natural way your arms move when you walk... very good... now add a little bounce to your steps... excellent! Now with some music!"

As a recording of the original Charleston music played, Sadie and Myrtle beamed at each other. They were actually doing it! The kicks were low and the bounces barely there, but they were keeping up nonetheless. Until Josie threw a curveball.

"Now it's time to get those feet and knees going! Heels out, toes out, heels in, toes in."

"All at the same time?" Sadie mouthed to Myrtle over the music. She could feel her confidence sinking.

Myrtle shrugged, the shoulder movement throwing everything else off kilter even more.

"And now hands on your knees! Follow me... cross... uncross... cross again, and so forth," Josie called out enthusiastically.

Sadie and Myrtle exchanged panicked glances as Josie demonstrated the "knocky knees" step with ease.

"I don't know about you," Sadie said, leaning toward Myrtle. "I can get my feet to work, my knees to work, and my hands to work, but not all at the same time."

Myrtle nodded in complete agreement.

"And now let's add the "waterfall," Josie continued, demonstrating a series of movements that both Sadie and Myrtle found —much to their delight—that they could do.

"Thank you, Simon Says!" Sadie exclaimed. "I always knew kindergarten would come in handy later in life!" She followed Josie by putting her palms together over her head, then dropping her hands to her shoulders before placing them on her knees.

Josie stopped the music and let students take a few deep breaths while she complimented everyone on their progress. "You're doing great, all of you!" She sent a smile in Sadie and Myrtle's direction.

"A look of approval!" Myrtle beamed.

"Or else of sympathy," Sadie said, grinning.

"And now, let's wrap this up with Charleston steps of your choice," Josie said. "Just have fun with it!"

Josie started the music again, and as a medley of "Five Foot Two, Eyes of Blue," "Ain't She Sweet," and "Yes, Sir, that's my Baby" filled the room, everyone began moving to the music, some sticking with basic steps, others creating more complicated combinations. Sadie and Myrtle stuck to the basics—with a little added boa flouncing—finding that most enjoyable. After all, the whole point in attending the class to begin with was to have fun.

When the lesson ended, they applauded with everyone else before going up to thank Josie.

"You two did great!" Josie said.

"Very kind of you," Myrtle said. "But oh my, putting all those steps together is quite a challenge!"

Sadie agreed. "Steps, kicks, knees, heels, toes, arms, hips, front, back, inside out, upside down..."

Josie laughed. "It just takes practice. You had a good time, right?"

"Yes!" Sadie and Myrtle exclaimed in unison.

"That's the most important thing." Josie looked up at a wall clock. "I'd better go get ready for the show. Oh, by the way, I put your names on the guest list for the after-party at the Blind Pig."

"How wonderful!" Sadie exclaimed. She and Myrtle exchanged looks and nodded.

"We look forward to it," Myrtle said.

After a few more words of thanks, Sadie and Myrtle deposited their accessories—reluctantly—on the back table and headed to their rooms to relax and refresh before the show that evening.

TWENTY-FOUR

"Ms. Kramer."

"Detective Broussard."

Sadie's favorite long-distance detective answered the phone on the third ring. As always, they greeted each other formally even though their relationship had evolved beyond formalities. They'd started off with these greetings, and the habit stuck. Sadie rather liked it.

"I didn't expect to hear from you while you and Myrtle tore up Las Vegas. I respect the sanctity of a girls weekend."

Sadie smiled, warmed by the sound of his voice. She could also hear the grin behind it. "I intended to keep the "no boys allowed" sign on the clubhouse, but Amber told me you called, and I'm extending the trip a couple of days, so I didn't want you to worry."

"Why on earth would I worry?" Broussard said. "Oh wait. Maybe because you always seem to find yourself in the middle of something unexpected. Which makes me afraid to ask how this trip is going."

"Well, I could tell you not to ask." Sadie had a sudden image of herself winding her finger around a phone cord as she would have done decades earlier.

Broussard cleared his throat. "Which tells me I should."

Sadie weighed this, finding herself in a unique position as opposed to other trips. The detective network was close-knit, and he often knew about events on her travels without her telling him. This time he didn't. But she was essentially busted now by virtue of the phone call, so she knew she needed to fill him in. And why mince words? She might as well just spit it out.

"Well, it's like this," Sadie began. "Myrtle got tickets to the show here at the hotel, VIP opening night tickets, in fact. But the show director was found deceased in his hotel room right before the show was to open."

Again Broussard cleared his throat. "Dare I ask who the unfortunate detective is that you have undoubtedly been pestering?"

"I wouldn't exactly say we've been pestering him..."

"Oh right. There's two of you. Poor guy. Double trouble."

Sadie sighed. "He seems like a decent guy. His name is Tanner. I mean, *Detective* Tanner, of course. Walks like Charlie Chaplin. It's rather endearing. Fits right in with hotel theme and time period."

"So tell me more about this. I haven't looked into anything outside of this area this week. We've been swamped with local cases, as usual."

Sadie wasn't at all surprised to hear this. As a detective in New Orleans, he usually had his hands full. She started from the beginning, from the announcement the stage manager made the night the show was scheduled to open, to the various production, casino, and hotel people, to bits and pieces of conversations, interactions, and details she'd picked up along the way.

"That's a good amount of information," Broussard said. "I'm impressed." Sadie could hear him tapping a pencil against his desk.

"I do my best," Sadie said. "I take this amateur detective stuff seriously."

"I know you do," Broussard admitted reluctantly. "So do you have any theories yet?"

"Actually, I think I know 'whodunnit,' as they say in the mystery world."

"Really? Then present your case, so to speak."

"Here's what I think and why." Sadie followed that with time-line details, potential suspects and relationships, an overview of the hotel, and things she'd heard or witnessed. She summed it up and waited for his response, which was longer in coming than she expected. She could hear papers shuffling. At one point, she asked if he was still on the line.

"I'm just looking over notes I've made while you were talking. You have some excellent points. I'm not exactly sure how you've managed to infiltrate the casino, theater, bar, buffet, and spa so thoroughly in a short amount of time, not to mention zip-lining and taking dance lessons, but I'm impressed."

"Thank you!" Sadie beamed at the praise.

"Take your theory to Tanner," Broussard said. "It's worth telling him what you think. It's reasonable. As reasonable as murder can be, of course."

"I'll do that," Sadie said. "Thank you."

"You're welcome. Oh, and Sadie?"

"Yes?"

"Maybe you need to solve your next case down here in New Orleans. I miss you."

Sadie had just ended the call when there was a knock at the door. *Perfect timing,* she thought. It took only a few strides to cross the room and open the door.

"Detective Tanner, just the person I want to see."

TWENTY-FIVE

The theater was buzzing with energy as Sadie and Myrtle entered. It was as if the excitement of the first night had quadrupled between the originally scheduled opening and this one. Heads tilted toward each other as audience members chattered in anticipation, excited that the show would finally open. Opening nights always carried a bit of extra thrill. Combined with the recent drama, this was guaranteed to be an extraordinary evening.

Sadie and Myrtle edged their way along the row to their seats, accompanied by subdued sounds of orchestra preparations: a riff off a snare drum, a triad of notes from a viola, the rich tone of a bassoon. They were thrilled to find once again that VIP gift bags waited on each seat.

"Aren't we lucky!" Myrtle exclaimed as she lifted the bag and sat down. She immediately began rummaging through it. "I wonder if these are the same as the other night. I wouldn't mind another complimentary spa treatment."

"And I wouldn't mind more of that imported chocolate," Sadie said as she took her seat and balanced her tote bag—Coco resting calmly inside—on her lap. She did a quick inventory of the

VIP gifts and grinned as she held up the desired confection. "Voilà!"

"Another etched shot glass," Myrtle said, holding up her own treasure. "Now I have a set!"

"And another drink coupon for the Blind Pig." Sadie waved the coupon in the air, delighted. "I've grown fond of those Mary Pickfords."

"You'll have to order one after the show," Myrtle said as she placed her bag of VIP goodies on her seat, wedging it between her hip and the arm rest. "Josie said we're invited to the after-party."

"Yes, we are. And believe me I'm looking forward to it," Sadie said, a mischievous expression on her face.

Myrtle eyed her expectantly. "I'm sure you are after everything you told me last night!"

"It should be an interesting evening to say the least!" Sadie also set her bag to the side, making sure to position the chocolate bar so it wouldn't get crushed.

"Doesn't taste the same if broken, hmm?" Myrtle teased, having seen the care Sadie took with the chocolate.

"Not at all!" Sadie exclaimed. As a chocolate connoisseur, she had her standards. Chocolate deserved to be handled with care.

The flurry of orchestra sounds faded away as the lights to the theater dimmed. The audience settled as a spotlight hit the curtain. Just as he had the ill-fated first night of the production opening, the stage manager took a place center stage. However, this night his expression was cheerful and stress-free as he thanked the audience for being there, both those who had retained tickets from the first night and those who now had tickets from previous refunds.

"We're delighted to have you all here! The Prohibition period was a time of exciting advancements in many industries, including automobiles, aviation, radio, music, and cinema. Silent films evolved into 'talkies,' and dance crazes and jazz music added pizzazz to evenings out at underground establishments known as speakeasies. This is what we celebrate tonight! So without further ado, welcome to *Bugsy's Juice Joint!*" He exited the stage as the spotlight disappeared.

Silence followed a quick double tap from a conductor's baton, and then cymbals crashed as the curtain lifted to reveal an exquisite set framed by billowing drapes of shimmering black and gold fabric tied back with tassels. A flashing neon sign proclaimed the stage as Bugsy's. A steep staircase ascended from the center of the stage toward the back, leading to an upper runway. Sparkling crystal chandeliers hung to each side. Art Deco tables and chairs dotted the areas near the wings. Two additional tables were whisked out by stagehands dressed in black to occupy corners of the apron. Shadows and spotlights highlighted different areas of the set. The overall effect was striking, giving the audience the sensation of being inside Bugsy's itself.

"Remarkable!" Myrtle whispered. "It's nothing like it looked during the rehearsal!"

"The magic of lighting and music," Sadie whispered back, equally impressed.

"And costumes," Myrtle added as a wave of rose and silver sequins took the stage. "How stunning!"

"Very Ziegfeld-esque!" Sadie exclaimed, delighted. "And look, there's Josie, third from the right." Sadie pointed her out as the orchestra struck up an introduction to "Second Hand Rose."

"What's on her head?" Myrtle exclaimed.

"Feathers," Sadie said.

"And more feathers!" Myrtle added.

"And even *more* feathers!" Sadie leaned forward, trying to take in the elaborate headpiece. "It seems to defy gravity."

"Agreed. It must be two feet high," Myrtle said. "Maybe three."

Sadie sat back. "I wonder how she can dance without it falling off."

"Carefully, I suspect." Myrtle raised both hands to her head as if straightening a similar headpiece on herself. "It must be *glued* on!"

Sadie contemplated this. "I think that would be impractical unless they wear the same outfit for the entire show."

"You're kidding, of course."

"Of course."

As if to prove Sadie's point, the dancers exited via a splendid swirl of movement up the staircase. After a short vaudeville-ish pantomime act sure to allow for costume changes, Josie and several of the other girls returned to the stage in more demure—though equally sparkly—outfits with cloche hats for a rendition of "Tea for Two."

The show continued as Sadie and Myrtle sat mesmerized by the music of the Prohibition era mixed with exquisite costumes and fascinating set changes. "Bye, Bye, Blackbird" brought a flurry of black feathers across the stage, and "It Don't Mean a Thing if It Ain't Got that Swing" featured bright red flapper costumes with enough swaying fringe—more fringe than fabric, but this was Vegas after all—to sweep the entire theater. A number set to "Puttin' on the Ritz" was so extravagantly decked out in gold splendor that it seemed they ought to be able to take it to the bank and cash it in.

As Sadie closed her eyes to appreciate the horn section's fervent enthusiasm, she felt Myrtle tap her arm and lean in to whisper.

"Look, over by the stage door!"

Sadie opened her eyes and glanced in that direction. Two men leaned against the wall, their heads tilted together. It took a moment to identify them in the dark, but a sconce gave off just enough light to do so.

"Looks like it's Bennett," Sadie whispered back to Myrtle. "And Asher, the new show director." She watched as Asher slipped inside the stage door, and Bennett exited up the side aisle.

"They don't look too pleased," Myrtle noted.

"You're right," Sadie agreed. "Interesting. The show's going well. The house is packed, and I heard it's sold out for weeks."

"Shhhh!" The hiss of a complaint came from the row behind them.

Myrtle and Sadie both sat up straight and remained quiet for a good thirty seconds before Sadie leaned in toward each other again.

"He's probably just pushing Asher about the budget the same way he was with Seth."

"Shhhh!"

Myrtle looked behind her and nodded an apology before leaning toward Sadie one last time. "You don't want to get thrown out of here, too, do you?"

"*Escorted* out," Sadie whispered before turning to the row behind them and mouthing, "*Sorry.*"

With that, Sadie sat back and enjoyed the remainder of the show, which wrapped up with a full cast sparkling white and gold extravaganza set to "42nd Street." Both Sadie and Myrtle jumped to their feet with the rest of the auditorium to give a standing ovation.

"What a fantastic show!" Myrtle exclaimed.

"Fabulous!" Sadie mirrored her enthusiasm, clapping wildly. Even Coco yipped along in agreement, though fortunately the tiny yaps could not be heard over the crowd.

"And now on to the party," Myrtle said as the audience began to exit the theater. "This should be interesting."

"Oh, indeed," Sadie said with a mysterious grin. "More interesting than expected, I'm quite sure."

TWENTY-SIX

Sadie applauded as Josie entered the bar. Out of costume and sans makeup now, Josie's casual jeans and sweatshirt made her look like just one of the crowd. But in Sadie's eyes, she was the exquisite, bright—and sometimes scantily clad—dancer who'd glowed like a bright light from the stage just an hour before.

"The show was fabulous," Sadie exclaimed.

"It really was!" Myrtle agreed enthusiastically. "I've never seen anything like it. I've always wanted to see a Las Vegas show, and it was everything I thought it would be and more. What a thrill!"

Sadie and Myrtle grabbed a side table as cast members continued to enter. As the bar became more crowded, the atmosphere was that of joy and relief that the show had finally opened after the unfortunate delay. More unfortunate for Seth than anyone, of course, but still a delay for all.

"I'm so glad Josie arranged for us to attend this party," Myrtle said. "That sign outside clearly says it's a private event." She took a sip of her Bee's Knees. "Are casino employees invited too?"

"Some are," Sadie said. "I see Brandi and Stacey on approach now. And Dylan is just behind them." She watched as the trio stepped into the bar. Brandi and Stacey began to mingle with the cast members while Dylan headed to the counter, presumably to order drinks.

Sadie looked around. "We'll be seeing Detective Tanner too. I spoke with him earlier, before the show. He'll be here."

Josie slid in beside Sadie and directed her to look at the door as the show's new director stepped in. "Get a load of that," she said, nodding toward an overly effusive Asher, accepting congratulations and pats on the back with a false modesty that was painfully obvious.

"It's as if he put on the whole show himself, isn't it?" Myrtle observed.

"Yep," Josie said. "That's exactly what he acts like. Pretty nervy if you ask me. Nothing tonight was his doing. The only thing that changed the past two days was us having to put up with his arrogance. Everything in the show is exactly as Seth set it."

"What about all those new notices on the board backstage that we saw at rehearsal?" Sadie asked.

Josie rolled her eyes. "Those weren't new. They were all Seth's notes, rewritten with a change here and there. Asher just made it look like they were all his."

Sadie turned her gaze to the bar, noticing that Dylan had moved to the end of the counter and was talking with Bennett, who was accompanied by his wife.

"Look who's over there talking with Dylan," Sadie said, nudging Myrtle with her elbow.

"And his wife is with him," Myrtle said, recognizing her from the elevator. "That's who got so upset when he gave me the tickets."

This should be interesting, Sadie thought.

"Bennett is so annoying," Josie said. "I don't know why he can't stay in his office. It's not like he's the director and has to be there." She stood up. "I'm off to make the rounds. Have fun!"

"Enjoy the party!" Sadie said, motioning with her hand as if shooing Josie away. "You've earned it!"

"Sounds like Bennett might be up to no good," Myrtle said as Josie walked away.

Sadie nodded. "I'm sure you're right, at least as far as finances go. I suspect he's going to get hit in the head with an audit in the near future. The *very* near future."

A burst of laughter came from a group of cast members near the bar, each with a shot glass in hand. Asher signaled for another round, and both Mason and another bartender nodded, each swamped already with other drink orders.

Brandi and Stacey had grabbed places at a center table. Dylan, having finished his conversation with Bennett, was just joining them with drinks for each.

"Everyone's having a good time," Sadie noted. "They've earned this." *It's a shame there's going to be a hiccup in the celebration,* she thought.

"And now look who's here," Myrtle said, nodding toward the door. Detective Tanner paused to speak with the doorman and then entered. The doorman made a quick trip to the bar to speak with Mason and then returned to his post.

"Perfect timing," Sadie said as she stood up. "Excuse me a moment, Myrtle. I believe we're about to have some extra entertainment."

"Like an encore." Myrtle grinned.

"Something like that!" Sadie crossed the room and stood by Tanner. "It's a shame to break up the party like this," she said, eager as she was to have the truth come out. "They're having such a great time."

"All part of the job," Tanner said as he and Sadie faced the room. The music cut out, and Tanner nodded a thank-you to the doorman.

Here goes, Sadie thought. She had an unsettling feeling as if expecting a bomb to go off. There was never a way to know how people would take unexpected news. And the more shocking it was, the more unpredictable the response could be.

Detective Tanner waited for the room to quiet down, which happened fairly rapidly as they noticed the police presence.

"I am sorry to break up the party. I know you've earned it," Tanner began. "And the reason for doing so doesn't apply to most of you, so I am especially sorry for that. But we have an update that I need to share. To be specific, we know who killed your director, Seth."

Gasps could be heard around the room, and Sadie searched the crowd to gauge reactions. The expressions were all of shock, even on those who should have appeared nervous at the announcement.

"Many of you had difficulties with him as your director," Tanner said. "Others with him personally. I'm going to let Ms. Kramer here explain." He gestured to Sadie, who took over.

"Asher," Sadie began, causing heads to whip around and stare as the new director's face paled.

"You resented Seth for getting the director job. You felt you should have been given it."

"Well, I should have!" Asher exclaimed. "Look at how great the show was tonight."

Several cast members laughed, and Josie spoke up. "Because of Seth! You only took over a show that was already set."

"And now you're the director," Sadie said. "You gained what you wanted by means of his death. But you didn't kill him."

"Of course not!" Asher looked both incensed and relieved. He crossed his arms and leaned back against the bar.

Tanner motioned for her to continue. She turned her attention to the table of casino employees.

"Dylan, you've had quite a bit of interaction with the police lately, including being taken down to the station more than once." Sadie saw Dylan and Tanner exchange glances. A few whispers passed through the crowd. "Some of that had to do with Seth indirectly. But you didn't kill him."

Sadie turned her attention to Bennett, who was beginning to look nervous. "Bennett..."

"How do you even know who I am?" Bennett exclaimed.

Josie laughed. "Everyone knows who you are, Bennett! You're everywhere, all the time!" Murmurs of agreement passed through the crowd.

"You and Seth had major disagreements over the show budget," Sadie continued. "In fact, it almost came to blows the afternoon the show was scheduled to open. When you went to see him in his room. Isn't that true?"

"That's ridiculous." Bennett swirled his drink and took a gulp. "Why would I go to his room?"

Tanner spoke up. "Your fingerprints were on a chair that had been tossed across the room as well as on a smashed lamp and a glass table."

Bennett sputtered as heads twisted in his direction. "Okay, we had a nasty fight. I'd gone to his room to tell him we couldn't approve additional funds that he'd been demanding. He was furious, and we argued. I lost my temper and tossed a few things around. But I didn't kill him! He was very much alive and still screaming at me when I left the room!"

"That's true," Sadie said as she turned to the table with Brandi and Stacey. "You didn't kill him. Stacey did." Brandi gasped and turned to Stacey, who sat perfectly still.

"Stacey?" Brandi whispered, eyes wide. "That can't be true!"

Bennett snapped his head in Stacey's direction. Others did the same, equally confused.

Suddenly Stacey flew from her seat. "It was an accident, I swear!" She turned to face Bennett. "I went to talk to Seth, to convince him not to turn you in! I did it for us!"

"I have no idea what you're talking about!" Bennett shouted.

"Seth was going to go to the authorities with dirt on you about finances!" Stacey pleaded. "It was going to destroy all our plans to be together! I couldn't let that happen!" She broke down crying. "Don't you understand?"

"I think *I* understand!" Bennett's wife fumed as she slapped her husband's face.

Stacey turned to Brandi. "You said that you'd told Seth the police had information about Bennett. You'd overheard it on a phone call Dylan was on."

Brandi shot Dylan an apologetic look, and he frowned.

"Seth was already upset from seeing you," Stacey continued, turning back to Bennett. "I'd never seen him so angry. He grabbed my shoulders and tried to convince me he had to turn you in, that you'd been stealing funds that should have gone to financing the show. I got scared and pushed him away, and he fell and hit his head on that glass table."

Detective Tanner raised his hand. "This is where I mention embezzling." He focused his gaze on Bennett.

Stacey collapsed back into her chair and covered her face, sobbing. Brandi hesitantly put her arm around her.

Tanner stepped forward. "I believe we should continue this down at the station."

Sadie noticed two officers had arrived and were standing in the doorway. They moved through the bar, one asking Stacey to accompany him, the other asking Bennett. Tanner followed, requesting that Brandi and Dylan accompany them to the station for questioning and clarification.

As they left—four employees, two officers, and one detective—Mason turned the music back on, and the stunned cast eased back into the party.

Sadie sat back down with Myrtle, and Josie joined them, shaking her head as she gave Sadie a pat on the back. And no one said anything. After all, pretty much everything had been said.

TWENTY-SEVEN

The lobby was busy but not crowded as Sadie and Myrtle sat at the coffee kiosk, luggage beside them. A late check-out arrangement had let them miss the morning departure crowd. Now just past noon, they enjoyed the relative peace while sipping coffee drinks.

"Quite the girls' getaway we've had, don't you think?" Sadie looked at Myrtle, eyebrows raised. "I didn't expect this much fun!"

Myrtle shook her head. "I'm beginning to think any trip with you is going to be filled with some sort of shenanigans. You were wrapped up in something like this when we met."

"Ah, yes, the celebrity that washed up on the beach." Sadie remembered it clearly. It was definitely a beach vacation gone sideways.

"When exactly did you know who the killer was this time?" Myrtle asked. "I've been trying to figure that out."

"It was when Brandi mentioned she'd told Stacey about overhearing Dylan's phone call," Sadie said. "I remembered how cozy Stacey and Bennett looked in the buffet that time."

"So you figured Stacey wanted to protect Bennett? That she would go to Seth to convince him not to turn him in?"

"That's the overall scenario," Sadie said. "Broussard thought it was a decent theory, too, when I talked to him. I trust his judgment. So I went to Tanner with it."

"And Tanner hadn't thought of that angle."

"No," Sadie said. "He didn't see Stacey and Bennett together, so he wouldn't have known they were involved. And even if he had, he didn't know about the phone call that Brandi overheard or that she'd told Stacey about it."

"I really thought for a while that Asher was the killer," Myrtle said. "He wanted that all along."

"It seemed like a possibility," Sadie agreed. "But it wasn't a strong enough motive. At least in my opinion."

"And Bennett?"

Sadie shook her head. "That was another possibility. He and Seth disagreed about the show budget, and Seth might have suspected Bennett was up to something shady with finances. But Bennett would want the show to go on for the ticket money to roll in. It doesn't make sense that he'd want the director out of the way. Not when that person was a source of money."

Myrtle nodded. "And if you want to play games with money, you need the money to come in. He only stood to lose with Seth gone."

"Exactly," Sadie said. "Though it did look odd that he passed those tickets off to you so hurriedly the same afternoon that Seth was killed. As if he just wanted to get out of there."

"True," Myrtle said. "And we now know he went to Seth's room right before that."

"Right. But his eagerness to get out was because he was upset from their argument, not because he killed him. When he left, Seth was very much alive."

"I get it now," Myrtle said. "He was furious from their fight. That's why he was so upset in the elevator when he handed me the tickets. And why his wife was so surprised when he did. Though I suppose not as surprised as she is now."

"Yes, I'm sure that's true," Sadie said. "A lot came out at that party last night."

The site of a familiar face caused the conversation to pause. Both Sadie and Myrtle smiled at the unique gait of the approaching detective.

"Good afternoon, ladies," Detective Tanner said. "I take it you two are leaving us." He indicated the suitcases.

"We are, indeed, Detective," Sadie said. "And I think I speak for both of us when I say we thank you for the marvelous entertainment while we were here." She looked at Myrtle, who nodded.

Detective Tanner looked back and forth between the two women. "Well, it pains me to say this, but I'm thankful for your help, challenging as it was at times." He reached into his back pocket and pulled something out.

Sadie's eyebrows lifted. "You're not arresting us, are you?" She'd seen untold number of television shows where handcuffs were retrieved in this manner.

"No, though I dare say the thought crossed my mind a couple of times," he said. "I'm rewarding you for your assistance. You may want to stand for this very important ceremony."

Not one to say no to an officer of the law, Sadie obliged, as did Myrtle. Tanner peeled a sticker off a paper backing and attached it to Sadie's sweater.

Myrtle gasped. "Junior detective!" Sadie attempted to look down, but the sticker was too close to her neckline to see. But once Tanner awarded Myrtle hers, she could see it plainly. The bright gold sticker was clearly in the shape of a badge and bore the words Junior Detective.

"I'm thrilled, Detective!" Sadie exclaimed as she and Myrtle both beamed. "And just how official are these wonderful badges?"

"Let's just say any schoolchildren who visit the precinct on field trips, have special events at their schools, or run into us when we're out and about receive these."

"Ah!" Sadie nodded. "Quite selective, I see. We're honored,

Detective. It's very thoughtful of you. Does this mean we're welcome back anytime to help solve cases?"

Detective Tanner fought back a grin. "Definitely not."

Sadie and Myrtle exchanged glances and sighed.

"I did have my doubts," Sadie admitted.

"Same here, to be honest," Myrtle said.

"And with that, I shall take my leave," Tanner said. Wishing them safe travels, he walked away as Sadie and Myrtle both watched.

"He really just needs a hat, mustache, and cane," Sadie mused.

"Maybe we should send him some props after we get home."

"Brilliant idea." Sadie could already imagine his delight when receiving them.

"Oh," Myrtle said. "I saw Brandi on my way down here. She said to tell you she was signing up for a medical technician course."

"Wonderful!" Sadie said. "She and I talked about that. I think it'll be great for her."

They gathered their luggage and walked outside just as an airport shuttle pulled up in front of the hotel.

"I love our new badges," Sadie said. "Broussard is going to be so impressed." She tapped her badge affectionately.

"I think that's questionable, my fellow junior detective," Myrtle said.

"You may be right about that," Sadie admitted with a smile.

"This really was quite the getaway."

"Yes, I agree. I rather hate to see it end," Sadie said, thinking back to the Charleston lessons, the *Bugsy's Juice Joint* production, the ragtime and jazz music, and the overall intrigue of the trip.

Myrtle nodded. "We'll just have to do it again."

"Indeed, we will," Sadie said as she watched the shuttle driver load their luggage into the van. "And now that we're officially junior detectives, we can *really* have some fun."

"I like the way you think."

"So, until next time?" Sadie said.

Myrtle smiled. "Until next time."

Acknowledgments

Sadie and Coco's Las Vegas adventure only evolved with the help of others along the way.

I owe heartfelt thanks to Annie Sarac at The Editing Pen for polishing up the rough edges of *A Flair for Vegas*. As always, Elizabeth Christy's keen insight with developmental issues is a blessing. Mariah Sinclair deserves credit for her amazing cover design. Feedback from beta readers Jay Garner and Karen Putnam always makes these stories better. I'm also thankful to the Georgetown Writers for listening to me chatter about this book time and time again. And Paul Sterrett's constant support and remarkable patience with my crazy writing process is commendable.

If Sadie's chocolate addiction has caused you to experience cravings, you're in luck. Kim Davis has generously contributed the Lucky Chocolate Truffles recipe at the end of the book. You'll many more delicious goodies at her blog, Cinnamon and Sugar and a Little Bit of Murder.

Above all, I'm grateful for the support of family, friends, and readers. Their encouragement allows Sadie and Coco to find new adventures.

Lucky Chocolate Truffles

(Submitted by Kim Davis, from Cinnamon and Sugar and a Little Bit of Murder)

Ingredients
 Truffles:
 • 1 14-ounce sweetened condensed milk
 • 16 ounces good-quality bittersweet chocolate chips or bars chopped into small pieces
 • 2 teaspoons vanilla extract
 • 1 teaspoon ground cinnamon
 • 1/4 teaspoon sea salt
 Garnish:
 • Your choice of cocoa powder, hot cocoa mix, nonmelting confectioners' sugar, or holiday-themed candy sprinkles

Instructions:
 1. Heat the sweetened condensed milk in a small saucepan just until the edges start to bubble. Don't bring to a boil.
 2. Place the chocolate in a medium-sized, heat-proof bowl. Pour the hot milk over the chocolate and allow to sit for two

minutes. Add the vanilla, sea salt, and cinnamon, and stir until the chocolate is fully melted.

3. Cover and refrigerate until chilled, around one hour.

4. Roll the chilled mixture into small balls, and then roll into your choice of garnish.

5. Serve truffles at room temperature. Store leftovers in the refrigerator.

Books by Deborah Garner

The Paige MacKenzie Series

Above the Bridge

When NY reporter Paige MacKenzie arrives in Jackson Hole, it's not long before her instincts tell her there's more than a basic story to be found in the popular, northwestern Wyoming mountain area. A chance encounter with attractive cowboy Jake Norris soon has Paige chasing a legend of buried treasure passed down through generations. Sidestepping a few shady characters who are also searching for the same hidden reward, she will have to decide who is trustworthy and who is not.

The Moonglow Café

The discovery of an old diary inside the wall of the historic hotel soon sends NY reporter Paige MacKenzie into the underworld of art and deception. Each of the town's residents holds a key to untangling more than one long-buried secret, from the hippie chick owner of a new age café to the mute homeless man in the town park. As the worlds of western art and sapphire mining collide, Paige finds herself juggling research, romance, and danger.

Three Silver Doves

The New Mexico resort of Agua Encantada seems a perfect destination for reporter Paige MacKenzie to combine work with well-deserved rest and relaxation. But when suspicious jewelry shows up on another guest, and the town's storyteller goes missing, Paige's R&R is soon redefined as restlessness and risk. Will an unexpected overnight trip to Tierra Roja Casino lead her to the answers she seeks, or are darker secrets lurking along the way?

Hutchins Creek Cache

When a mysterious 1920s coin is discovered behind the Hutchins Creek Railroad Museum in Colorado, Paige MacKenzie starts digging into four generations of Hutchins family history, with a little help from the Denver Mint. As legends of steam engines and coin mintage mingle, will Paige discover the true origin of the coin, or will she find herself riding the rails dangerously close to more than one long-hidden town secret?

Crazy Fox Ranch

As Paige MacKenzie returns to Jackson Hole, she has only two things on her mind: enjoy life with Wyoming's breathtaking Grand Tetons as the backdrop and spend more time with handsome cowboy Jake Norris as he prepares to open his guest ranch. But when a stranger's odd behavior leads her to research Western filming in the area—in particular, the movie Shane, will it simply lead to a freelance article for the Manhattan Post, or will it lead to a dangerous, hidden secret?

Sweet Sierra Gulch

Paige MacKenzie isn't convinced there's anything "sweet" about Sweet Sierra Gulch when she arrives in the small California Gold Rush town. Still, there's plenty of history as well as anticipated romance with her favorite cowboy, Jake Norris. But when the owner of the local café goes missing, Paige is determined to find out why. Will she uncover a dangerous secret in the town's old mining tunnels, or will curiosity land her in over her head?

The Sadie Kramer Flair Series

A Flair for Chardonnay

When flamboyant senior sleuth Sadie Kramer learns the owner of her favorite chocolate shop is in trouble, she heads for the California wine country with a tote-bagged Yorkie and a slew of questions. The fourth generation Tremiato Winery promises answers but not before a dead body turns up at the vintners' scheduled Harvest Festival. As Sadie juggles truffles, tips, and turmoil, she'll need to sort the grapes from the wrath in order to find the identity of the killer.

A Flair for Drama

When a former schoolmate invites Sadie Kramer to a theatre production, she jumps at the excuse to visit the Monterey Bay area for a weekend. Plenty of action is expected on stage, but when the show's leading lady turns up dead, Sadie finds herself faced with more than one drama to follow. With both cast members and production crew as potential suspects, will Sadie and her sidekick Yorkie, Coco, be able to solve the case?

A Flair for Beignets

With fabulous music, exquisite cuisine, and rich culture, how could a week in New Orleans be anything less than fantastic for Sadie Kramer and her sidekick Yorkie, Coco? And it is… until a customer at a popular patisserie drops dead face-first in a raspberry-almond tart. A competitive bakery, a newly formed friendship, and even her hotel's luxurious accommodations offer possible suspects. As Sadie sorts through a gumbo of interconnected characters, will she discover who the killer is, or will the killer discover her first?

A Flair for Truffles

Sadie Kramer's friendly offer to deliver three boxes of gourmet Valentine's Day truffles for her neighbor's chocolate shop backfires when she arrives to find the intended recipient deceased. Even more intriguing is the fact that the elegant heart-shaped gifts were ordered by three different men. With the help of one detective and the hindrance of another, Sadie will search San Francisco for clues. But will she find out "whodunit" before the killer finds a way to stop her?

A Flair for Flip-Flops

When the body of a heartthrob celebrity washes up on the beach outside Sadie Kramer's luxury hotel suite, her fun in the sun soon turns into sleuthing with the stars. The resort's wine and appetizer gatherings, suspicious guest behavior, and casual strolls along the beach boardwalk may provide clues, but will they be enough to discover who the killer is, or will mystery and mayhem leave a Hollywood scandal unsolved?

A Flair for Goblins

When Sadie Kramer agrees to help decorate for San Francisco's high-society Halloween shindig, she expects to find whimsical ghosts, skeletons, and jack- o-lanterns when she shows up at the Wainwright Mansion—not a body. With two detectives, a paranormal investigator turned television star, and a cauldron full of family members cackling around her, Sadie and her sidekick Yorkie are determined to find out who the killer is. Will an old superstition help lead to the truth? Or will this simply become one more tale in the mansion's haunted history?

A Flair for Shamrocks

When flamboyant senior sleuth Sadie Kramer's car breaks down outside a small beach town, the repair lands her in unexpected lodging above an Irish pub for St. Patrick's Day. With pub games, green beer, and a potbellied pig named Paddy in the mix, it's bound to be a unique holiday. An assortment of local characters could be guilty, but only one is the killer. Sadie and her sidekick Yorkie will need the luck of the Irish to solve the mystery.

A Flair for Vegas

When Sadie Kramer meets up with her friend Myrtle for a girls' getaway in Las Vegas, they're especially thrilled when VIP tickets to the hotel's sold-out production of Bugsy's Juice Joint unexpectedly fall into their hands. That is until the body of the show's director is found in his hotel room. With suspects spread throughout the hotel, casino, and theater, Sadie and Myrtle have some sleuthing to do. Add in Coco's typical Yorkie antics, and it's bound to be a weekend no one will forget. Will Sadie manage to solve this mystery? Or will what happens in Vegas stay in Vegas this time?

The Moonglow Christmas Series

Mistletoe at Moonglow

The small town of Timberton, Montana, hasn't been the same since resident chef and artist, Mist, arrived, bringing a unique new age flavor to the old western town. When guests check in for the holidays, they bring along worries, fears, and broken hearts, unaware that Mist has a way of working magic in people's lives. One thing is certain: no matter how cold winter's grip is on each guest, no one leaves Timberton without a warmer heart.

Silver Bells at Moonglow

Christmas brings an eclectic gathering of visitors and locals to the Timberton Hotel each year, guaranteeing an eventful season. Add in a hint of romance, and there's more than snow in the air around the small Montana town. When the last note of Christmas carols has faded away, the soft whisper of silver bells from the front door's wreath will usher guests and townsfolk back into the world with hope for the coming year.

Gingerbread at Moonglow

The Timberton Hotel boasts an ambiance of near-magical proportions during the Christmas season. As the aromas of ginger, cinnamon, nutmeg, and molasses mix with heartfelt camaraderie and sweet romance, holiday guests share reflections on family, friendship, and life. Will decorating the outside of a gingerbread house prove easier than deciding what goes inside?

Nutcracker Sweets at Moonglow

When a nearby theater burns down just before Christmas, cast members of *The Nutcracker* arrive at the Timberton Hotel with only a sliver of holiday joy. Camaraderie, compassion, and shared inspiration combine to help at least one hidden dream come true. As with every Christmas season, this year's guests will face the New Year with a renewed sense of hope.

Snowfall at Moonglow

As holiday guests arrive at the Timberton Hotel with hopes of a white Christmas, unseasonably warm weather hints at a less-than-wintery wonderland. But whether the snow falls or not, one thing is certain: with resident artist and chef, Mist, around, there's bound to be a little magic. No one ever leaves Timberton without renewed hope for the future.

Yuletide at Moonglow

When a Yuletide festival promises jovial crowds, resident artist and chef, Mist, knows she'll have her hands full. Between the legendary Christmas Eve dinner at the Timberton Hotel and this season's festival events, the unique magic of Christmas in this small Montana town offers joy, peace, and community to guests and townsfolk alike. As always, no one will return home without a renewed sense of hope for the future.

Starlight at Moonglow

As the Christmas holiday approaches, a blizzard threatens the peaceful ambiance that the Timberton Hotel usually offers its guests. Even resident artist and chef, Mist, known to work near miracles, has no control over the howling winds and heavy snowfall. But there's always a bit of magic in this small Montana town, and this year's storm may just find it's no match for heartfelt camaraderie, joyful inspiration, and sweet romance.

Joy at Moonglow

Each holiday season is unique in the small Montana town of Timberton. New and returning guests bring their dreams, cares, and worries, and always leave with lighter hearts and renewed hope for the future. But no season has ever been as special as this one. Because, to everyone's delight, wedding bells will be ringing. Thanks to the heartfelt efforts of many and no shortage of sweet romance, this year will be the most joyful of all.

Evergreen Wishes at Moonglow

Christmas in the small town of Timberton, Montana, is always filled with holiday traditions, exquisite cuisine, and heartfelt camaraderie. When a majestic evergreen tree is placed in the center of town, inviting ornaments containing wishes, townsfolk and visitors are soon pondering what their hopes and dreams might be. Although wishes can't always come true, some just might with a bit of holiday magic.

Angels at Moonglow

The small Montana town of Timberton always provides a joyful Christmas retreat for visitors as well as those who live in the area. This year, an angel ornament project offers guests and local townsfolk a chance to reflect on others in their lives. As always, time spent together, exquisite food, and camaraderie allow guests a chance to trade worries for a sense of peace and hope for the future.

Sleigh Bells at Moonglow

Christmas in the small Montana town of Timberton is always filled with wonder as well as heartfelt camaraderie, exquisite cuisine, and holiday cheer. An old-fashioned sleigh ride through the forest this year promises to add plenty of joy for both visitors and townsfolk. Add to that the traditional Christmas Eve feast, the yearly cookie exchange, and resident artist and chef Mist's unique way of bringing inspiration to the season, and it's guaranteed to be a holiday to cherish.

Additional Titles

Cranberry Bluff

Molly Elliott's quiet life is disrupted when routine errands land her in the middle of a bank robbery. Accused and cleared of the crime, she flees both media attention and mysterious, threatening notes to run a bed-and-breakfast on the Northern California coast. Her new beginning is peaceful until five guests show up at the inn, each with a hidden agenda. As true motives become apparent, will Molly's past come back to haunt her, or will she finally be able to leave it behind?

Sweet Treats: Recipes from the Moonglow Christmas Series

Delicious recipes, including Glazed Cinnamon Nuts, Cherry Pecan Holiday Cookies, Chocolate Peppermint Bark, Cranberry Drop Cookies, White Christmas Fudge, Molasses Sugar Cookies, Lemon Crinkles, Spiced Apple Cookies, Swedish Coconut Cookies, Double-Chocolate Walnut Brownies, Blueberry Oatmeal Cookies, Cocoa Kisses, and more!

More Sweet Treats: Recipes from the Moonglow Christmas Series

Delicious recipes, including Chocolate Crinkle Cookies, Amish Sugar Cookies, Yuletide Coconut Cherry Cookies, Almond Crunch Bars, Chai Tea Shortbread Cookies, Peanut Butter Chocolate Fudge, Peppermint Snowball Cookies, Cranberry Walnut Pinwheels, Gingerbread Kiss Cookies, Eggnog Cookies with Rum Butter Icing, Glazed Fruitcake Cookies, Dutch Letter Almond Bars, Crème Brûlée Cookies, Caramel Apple Cookies, Date Nut Torte Squares, and more!

For more information on Deborah Garner's books:

Facebook:
   https://www.facebook.com/deborahgarnerauthor

Twitter:
   https://twitter.com/PaigeandJake

Website:
   http://deborahgarner.com

Mailing List:
   http://bit.ly/deborahgarner

www.ingramcontent.com/pod-product-compliance
Lightning Source LLC
Chambersburg PA
CBHW021711190726
48289CB00008B/2484